MW01001119

SIX DANCE LESSONS IN SIX WEEKS

by

Richard Alfieri

SAMUEL FRENCH, INC.

45 West 25th Street   7623 Sunset Boulevard
NEW YORK 10010   HOLLYWOOD 90046
LONDON   *TORONTO*

ISBN 0 573 60279 4   Printed in U.S.A.   #21510

IMPORTANT BILLING AND CREDIT REQUIREMENTS

All producers of *SIX DANCE LESSONS IN SIX WEEKS* *must* give credit to the Author of the Play in all programs distributed in connection with performances of the Play and in all instances in which the title of the Play appears for purposes of advertising, publicizing or otherwise exploiting the Play and/or a production. The name of the Author *must* appear on a separate line on which no other name appears, immediately following the title, and *must* appear in size of type not less than fifty percent the size of the title type.

World Premiere - June 6, 2001

GEFFEN PLAYHOUSE

Gilbert Cates	Randall Arney	Stephen Eich
Producing Director	*Artistic Director*	*Managing Director*

present

Six Dance Lessons
in Six Weeks

by

Richard Alfieri

with

Uta Hagen   David Hyde Pierce

Scenery by	Costumes by	Lighting by
Roy Christopher	**Helen Butler**	**Tom Ruzika**

Sound by	Dances Staged by	Production Stage Manager
Philip G. Allen	**Kay Cole**	**Alice Elliott Smith**

Directed by

Arthur Allan Seidelman

◉BELASCO THEATRE

111 West 44th Street
A Shubert Organization Theatre

Gerald Schoenfeld, *Chairman*   **Philip J. Smith,** *President*

Robert E. Wankel, *Executive Vice President*

RODGER HESS, MARCIA SELIGSON, ENTPRO PLAYS INC.
CAROLYN S. CHAMBERS, SIGHT SOUND AND ACTION, LTD.,
BRANTLEY M. DUNAWAY, JUDY ARNOLD, AND PATRICIA GREENWALD

present

POLLY BERGEN   and   MARK HAMILL

in

SIX DANCE LESSONS IN SIX WEEKS

by

RICHARD ALFIERI

Scenic Design	Costume Design	Lighting Design	Sound Design
ROY CHRISTOPHER	HELEN BUTLER	TOM RUZIKA	PHILIP G. ALLEN

Additional Casting by	Production Stage Manager	Technical Supervisor
CINDI RUSH CASTING	JIM SEMMELMAN	LARRY MORLEY

Marketing	Press Representative	General Management
LEANNE SCHANZER PROMOTIONS, INC.	BONEAU/BRYAN-BROWN	RICHARDS/CLIMAN, INC.

Associate Producers
MARILYN GILBERT, NATHAN RUNDLETT, ETELVINA HUTCHINS, SCOTTIE HELD
and JOSEPH M. EASTWOOD

Dances Choreographed by
KAY COLE

Directed by
ARTHUR ALLAN SEIDELMAN

CAST
(in order of appearance)

LILY HARRISON

MICHAEL MINETTI

The play is set in Lily Harrison's condo in St. Petersburg Beach, Florida.

Time
is the present

WEEK ONE — THE SWING
WEEK TWO — THE TANGO
WEEK THREE — THE VIENNESE WALTZ
WEEK FOUR — THE FOXTROT

Intermission

WEEK FIVE — THE CHA-CHA
WEEK SIX — CONTEMPORARY DANCE
WEEK TEN — BONUS LESSON

Scene 1

WEEK ONE — THE SWING

(The homogenized strains of a FORTIES SWING TUNE* RISE as
CURTAIN RISES on LILY HARRISON'S condominium high
above the Gulf of Mexico in St. Petersburg Beach, Florida.
This is a cookie-cutter unit, sold furnished and adamantly
designed to indicate tropical leisure -- from the bird-of-para-
dise motif on the drapes to the rattan swivel chair, settee
couch, and faux palms. Older pieces of furniture and bric-a-
brac from a previous existence are conspicuous as they try
unsuccessfully to coexist among the matching tropicalia. But
nature transports this contrived space from the pedestrian to
the spectacular: the upstage living room wall is dominated by
a wide picture window through which a projected image of the
Gulf creates a fantastic moving backdrop that starts as a sun-
lit blue sky and shimmering sea and metamorphoses into a
vibrant orange sunset by scene end.
The rattan swivel chair has been pushed R from the center of the
living room. A downstage carpet has been rolled up and
tucked against the chair.
Left of the living room a short bar with stools juts from the US wall
and borders the kitchen L. Refrigerator and kitchen counter with
sink are visible UL. A DL hallway leads to a bedroom off L.

Right of the living room is a small foyer and front door adjoining
     an exterior hallway. A bookcase and desk are built into the
     wall US of the foyer.
As DOORBELL RINGS, SWING TUNE FADES and LILY calls
     from Off L:)

     LILY. *(OS)* Coming! *(LILY HARRISON enters primping nerv-*
ously from the DL hallway. She is an attractive woman, slim, well-
coiffed and well, if conservatively, dressed — looking several years
younger than her actual seventy-two. She crosses to the foyer,
stops, takes a deep breath to compose herself, then looks intently
through the peep hole in the front door. The SWING TUNE FADES
OUT as:) Who is it?

     MICHAEL. *(OS)* The Dangerous Stranger!

(LILY pulls away from the peep hole in consternation.)

     LILY. What?!
     MICHAEL. *(OS)* Just kidding.
     LILY. Well *I'm* not. Who is it?!
     MICHAEL. *(OS)* It's Michael Minetti, Mrs. Harrison.
     LILY. From what company?!
     MICHAEL. *(OS)* Oh! Six Dance Lessons in Six Weeks!

(Lily quickly checks her face one last time in the foyer mirror, then
     opens the door to find MICHAEL MINETTI, an attractive man
     of forty-five trying to look thirty-five. Although still far from
     paunchy, Michael wears dress slacks and a shirt clearly pur-
     chased a few pounds ago. He combs his hair to hide a reced-
     ing hairline. He carries a small tote in one hand.)

LILY. Please come in!

MICHAEL. You sure?

LILY. *(Ushering him in.)* Yes. I'm sorry. I'm always very cautious when my husband isn't home.

MICHAEL. A lot of crime in St. Petersburg Beach? Pirates maybe?

LILY. A woman alone — even temporarily, that is — can't be too careful.

MICHAEL. I understand. Well, time's up. That'll be fifty dollars for the first lesson. *(Before LILY can register surprise:)* Just kidding. Boy are you easy. *(Looking out picture window.)* Wow! Great view! It's a poem — a little haiku to luxury and comfort. Have you lived here long?

LILY. My husband and I moved here from South Carolina — six years ago.

MICHAEL. *(Crossing to window.)* We live in Clearwater, but not at the beach.

LILY. You and your wife?

MICHAEL. *(Turning, hesitant, then:)* Yeah.... And of course I rarely see the Gulf from fourteen floors up. These ugly high-rises may ruin the view for the rest of us, but they're sure great from the inside. *(Then, turning suddenly.)* Oh, no offense.

LILY. *(Hiding her annoyance.)* None taken. I didn't build this place. Can I offer you something to drink?

MICHAEL. Oh, thanks. Just some water, please.

LILY. *(Crossing to kitchen.)* Should I pay you now? I mean, for the first lesson?

MICHAEL. Yes. On the mantle, like a hooker. I'm not putting out until I see some cashola. *(LILY turns at the refrigerator.)* Oh sorry, no offense.

LILY. None taken — *again.*

MICHAEL. You have to get used to my sense of humor.
LILY. Do I?

(MICHAEL silently castigates himself as he opens his tote and removes some CD's and a portable player.)

MICHAEL. Where can I plug this in?

(LILY returns with a glass of water.)

LILY. There's an outlet by the desk. I pushed the furniture back. Is that enough room?

(As he sets up the player and puts in a disc:)

MICHAEL. Plenty. So you know we're starting with the Swing — which became popular, you may recall, during World War II — a social reaction to the impending destruction of the world. Why follow rigid dance steps when you could be annihilated any second? Forget the cotillion and point me to the dance hall, booze, horny GI's and loose women. Relax, let your hair down, and make public reference to your genitals while you jiggle on the dance floor. Of course, Jitterbug and Rock & Roll are descendants of Swing, so critics may have been right in theorizing that it would lead to our moral downfall. *(He turns to LILY, who stands rather cold and rigid with his glass of water in hand.) You* don't ascribe to that theory, do you, Mrs. Harrison?
LILY. Whether I do or not, Mr. Minetti, I find myself wondering if I'm obliged to pay to listen to your two-bit sociologic commentary on the dances you teach.
MICHAEL. Not a cent. Certainly not two bits.

LILY. Thank you. Here's your water.

MICHAEL. *(Accepting glass.)* Thanks. But if it slips out, I'll just extend your time at the end of the lesson. See? It's completely complimentary -- and involuntary. *(MICHAEL takes a plastic vial from his pocket, unscrews it, tosses some pills into his mouth, and washes them down with water. Off LILY'S look:)* My vitamins. *(MICHAEL then removes some black and white vinyl "footprints" from his tote and begins tossing them around the floor.)* Now the dance, although rather free-form, does have definite steps and patterns — thank God, otherwise who needs *me* -- *(MICHAEL looks to LILY for a reaction; she replies with a jaundiced expression. He continues:)* Okay.... And I'll indicate these to you with these footprints, left foot black, right foot white —

LILY. You never answered my question about paying you now or at the end of the lesson.

MICHAEL. Is it really that important?

LILY. It is to me.

MICHAEL. Well, if you're not going to be able to concentrate until you —

LILY. It's not a question of my inability to —

MICHAEL. I mean, if you have this deep obsessive-compulsive need write a check *right now* —

LILY. I simply want to know what's done!

MICHAEL. I don't know what's done! This is my first fucking lesson you tight-assed old biddy! *(MICHAEL and LILY pass through a momentary Ice Age, then LILY turns abruptly and walks to the phone.)* Oh, gee, Mrs. Harrison, I'm really sorry for that little outburst.

LILY. Oh, "no offense," right?

(She consults her telephone pad and begins dialing a number.)

MICHAEL. Exactly — no offense. I had a really bad day — week, in fact. Who are you calling, Mrs. Harrison, may I ask?

LILY. *(Ignoring him, into receiver:)* Hello, is this the office of Six Dance Lessons in Six Weeks...?

MICHAEL. *(Crossing to her.)* Oh no, Mrs. Harrison. Please...

LILY. *(Continuing, with a pointed glance at MICHAEL.)* Good. I'd like to speak to the manager, please....Thank you.

MICHAEL. Oh, please don't, Mrs. Harrison. Please give me one last chance.

LILY. You just took it.

MICHAEL. Come on, there's always another last chance.

LILY. Not for you. I'll have to ask you to leave.

MICHAEL. Oh, no, Mrs. Harrison, we haven't even begun yet. We just got off on the wrong foot, so to speak —

LILY. Something tells me you spend all day on that foot. You know, Mr. Minetti, when I was teaching school I had a student like you once.

MICHAEL. Oh, really?

LILY. Yes, he was stoned to death by the other students at recess!

MICHAEL. Look, I said I'm sorry! Do I have to wax your goddamn floor?! *(LILY stares at MICHAEL, who is immediately remorseful.)* Oh, God, I did it again, didn't I.

LILY. *(Into receiver.)* Yes, Mr. Cunard, this is Lily Harrison — *(MICHAEL suddenly presses the flash button on the phone, ending the call. LILY turns to him, astonished.)* You hung up on me!

MICHAEL. *For* you! I just wanted a moment to explain and then, if you want to call Mr. Cunard, you can. *(As LILY begins dialing again, MICHAEL continues, speaking faster:)* You see, I think if you really understood the circumstances you'd cut me a little slack here. You seem like a compassionate woman, Mrs. Harrison...I mean, not really, but in case I'm wrong, I want you to know I need this job, like in *A Chorus Line* — did you see that show? — I *really* need this job —

LILY. Hello, Mr. Cunard, please — *(Then, with a hateful glance at MICHAEL.)* I was cut off.

MICHAEL. And in a way it was your fault. Even before I walked in the door you were unkind to me.

LILY. Call it a premonition.

MICHAEL. And I'm intensely sensitive to human contact, Mrs. Harrison. The slightest encounters leave me bruised or bleeding from invisible wounds. Like stigmata on my soul.

LILY. I see: Jesus meets Arthur Murray. Maybe you're too sensitive to work with the public, Mr. Minetti.

MICHAEL. Oh, how cavalierly you say that, Mrs. Harrison. We have no money, and...my wife's been very ill. Frankly, Mrs. Harrison, I don't know if she's going to survive!

(LILY stops and turns to MICHAEL, who has finally gotten her attention.)

LILY. *(Into receiver.)* One moment, please, Mr. Cunard. *(She presses the receiver to her breast and turns to MICHAEL.)* I'm warning you. I taught school for thirty years and I could write the definitive guide to spotting B.S.

MICHAEL. I couldn't lie about this. My wife's the bread winner in the house. And she hasn't been able to work for months. And now I'm afraid they're going to cancel her health coverage. This job is all the income we have.

LILY. *(Into receiver.)* Please hold, Mr. Cunard. *(To MICHAEL.)* What does your wife do?

MICHAEL. She's a veterinarian.

LILY. Where?

MICHAEL. The Seminole Cat, Dog, Bird, and Snake Hospital.

LILY. *Bird* and *snake?*

MICHAEL. *(Shrugging)* Could I make that up?

LILY. *(Into receiver.)* I'm sorry, I dialed the wrong number, Mr. Cunard.... Your name? Lucky guess.

(As she replaces the receiver, MICHAEL sags with relief.)

MICHAEL. Thank you.

LILY. Mr. Minetti, I know we're supposed to accept people the way they are, but in your case I find it *extremely* difficult.

MICHAEL. Oh, I know. I apologize. I'm not myself these days. The real me is more relaxed.

LILY. Please bring him with you next time. Or increase the dosage on your *ritalin.*

MICHAEL. Yes, Ma'am.

LILY. Now let's get on with it — my husband will be home soon. And I'm warning you, this is just a trial period for you.

MICHAEL. I know, and I appreciate it. You're very understanding, and I —

LILY. Oh, don't wear it out. Swing, you were saying, was invented by and for degenerates during World War II.

MICHAEL. Precisely! Now you've got the background, and that's so important, you know, for capturing the soul of the dance. That's really what you communicate when you dance — the soul. The steps are just conveyances, physical dialogue.

LILY. *(Smiling)* I like that image.

MICHAEL. *(Pleased)* Good. Of course, without the steps — *(Crosses to the CD player.)* You're just a stupid cow bouncing around on the dance floor.

(MICHAEL flicks on the CD player; A SWING TUNE* fills the room.)

LILY. I like that one less. But it's an incentive.

(MICHAEL takes LILY'S right hand in his left.)

MICHAEL. Exactly. Now, we're going to take eight small steps — all on the ball of the foot with a flexed knee. Starting with the *triple step,* which is three steps in any direction, starting to your right on *one-two-three, one-two-three.*

(As MICHAEL begins to move, LILY follows effortlessly, gracefully. MICHAEL looks at her, amazed.)

MICHAEL. Way to go, Mrs. Harrison! You were holding out on me!

LILY. This is the music of my youth, Mr. Minetti!

MICHAEL. Michael, please. This puts us on a first-name basis.

LILY. *(Girlish)* Alright — I'm Lily.

MICHAEL. Go, Lily! Now *fallaway rock* — right foot back in fallaway position, then rock forward on your left foot. That's it! You've got it!

LILY. Got it? I *had* it fifty years ago! *(The PHONE RINGS. LILY stops and gestures to the CD player.)* Would you mind?

(MICHAEL crosses to the CD player and snaps the MUSIC OFF.)

MICHAEL. Too bad. We were hitting the zone.

*For information regarding music use, please see page 85

LILY. *(Lifting the receiver.)* Hello.... Yes, hello, Ida.... *(Cupping receiver and whispering to MICHAEL.)* The woman downstairs. *(Into receiver again.)* No, Ida, the Andrews Sisters are not visiting me.... No I'm not bowling, I'm dancing....The covenants don't prevent me from dancing in my own unit....Well, if you'd like to pay for wall-to-wall carpeting, I'd love to have it. Beige would be nice.... *(Angrily)* Look, Ida, can the hollow threats and I'll just turn the music down, okay?! *(Then, suddenly smiling, friendly.)* No, the group trip to Epcot is the twenty-first....I know, I *love* the food in Morocco...! Okay! See you then. 'Bye!

(As she hangs up the receiver:)

MICHAEL. *(Confused)* That ended surprisingly well.

LILY. She's a lonely old woman suffering all the infirmities of old age except, unfortunately, hearing loss. By the end of the conversation she's forgotten why she called.

MICHAEL. But she remembered Epcot.

LILY. Seems silly, doesn't it — building your life around trips to the theme park, the beauty parlor, or the book store. We're people trying to make a day for ourselves. If we string enough together we have a week. Four of those and we've made it through a month. It's not silly — it's *survival.*

MICHAEL. I'm not passing judgement. But you're not old enough to consider yourself one of those people.

LILY. Sixty-eight. Card-carrying member of the "tight-assed old biddy" society.

MICHAEL. You're not going to throw *that* in my face, are you?

LILY. Whenever possible.

MICHAEL. Besides, you have your husband.

LILY. Yes.... Speaking of which, he'll be home soon and I'm

talking my time away.

MICHAEL. *(Crossing to the CD player.)* The meter stops for conversation.

LILY. Thank you.

MICHAEL. Oh, and, by the way, in case you were wondering, you can pay me at the end of the lesson. No gratuities accepted.

LILY. None offered — none earned.

MICHAEL. *(Snapping ON MUSIC.) Yet!* Those are fighting words, Lily! *(He struts toward LILY, and she sashays into his arms.)* Okay, you loose GI groupie, let's boogie! *(He spins LILY like a top and pulls her back into his arms. She squeals with delight, and:)* You're cookin' now...! Oh, Lily, you're waking up in the barracks tomorrow!

(As LIGHTS DIM, LILY cries out, and you might think you heard a girl of eighteen laughing. MUSIC CONTINUES as MICHAEL and LILY dance in silhouette in front of a RICH SUNSET BACKDROP through the picture window. As MICHAEL and LILY disappear from view, only the backdrop is visible.
The BACKDROP BEGINS TO LIGHTEN, SWING MUSIC FADES OUT, and:)

WEEK TWO — THE TANGO

(TANGO MUSIC* RISES and LIGHTS COME UP to reveal LILY sitting on the couch, tightly-wound with a troubled expression on her face. The BACKDROP INDICATES LATE AFTER-NOON ON A CLOUDY DAY.
The DOORBELL RINGS, and LILY rises with a start and crosses to the front door as MUSIC FADES OUT. LILY looks through the peep hole, then calls out:)

LILY. Who is it?
MICHAEL. *(OS)* Ted Bundy. I know you can see me through that thing.

(Unamused, LILY opens the door and barely looks at MICHAEL as he enters carrying his tote. He is dressed in black slacks and shirt.)

LILY. You can't always rely on your vision at my age.
MICHAEL. If that's a plea for sympathy, it's wasted on me. *(Continuing with Spanish accent.)* Are you ready to tango? Look, I dressed appropriately for the occasion — *(Gesturing out window.)* And even nature, she has cooperated with moody skies. *(Refusing his humor, LILY stares sternly at MICHAEL.)* And Lily, she looks a little moody herself. Perhaps she needs the seduction

of the dance to open her heart.
(MICHAEL strikes a dramatic dance pose; LILY ignores him.)

LILY. It's going to take more than that.

MICHAEL. *(Dropping his pose.)* What?

LILY. I'm not sure I want to continue these lessons.

MICHAEL. Did you have an acid flashback to our argument?

LILY. There was more than one; but no, I'm just not sure I want to associate with a *liar.*

MICHAEL. Alright, Lily, what's going on?

LILY. There is no Seminole Cat, Dog, Bird, and Snake Hospital!

MICHAEL. You checked?!

LILY. That's not the point! You lied to me! And the worst kind of lie — the one that appeals to compassion —-

MICHAEL. Which you're suppressing quite effectively today, I might add.

LILY. Your wife probably isn't sick, either, is she?

MICHAEL. You wouldn't *want* her to be, would you?

LILY. In fact, you don't even *have* a wife, do you?

(MICHAEL shakes his head "No.")

MICHAEL. Not even a little one.

LILY. How *could* you?

MICHAEL. Well, I figured if —

LILY. That was rhetorical! I feel so betrayed. Didn't we develop a rapport? *(MICHAEL stares blankly at LILY. LILY continues impatiently:)* Well, answer me, didn't we?!

MICHAEL. Oh, I thought *that* was rhetorical, too. Yes, we *did* develop a rapport. Yes, I *did* lie to you — but that was *before* we developed a rapport. I didn't lie about needing the job, Lily.

LILY. Necessity is no excuse for opportunism!

MICHAEL. Did you tack that homily on the bulletin board when you were teaching?! Because I'd like a copy to send to the bank instead of my mortgage payment.

LILY. You don't bend your ethics to suit the situation!

MICHAEL. That'll be the P.S. The bank especially loves it when I'm ethical.

LILY. I'm surprised your cynicism doesn't rise like a snake and choke you!

MICHAEL. Oh, save it for when your shoes don't match your purse!

(MICHAEL begins gathering his things. LILY seems dismayed by the finality of it.)

LILY. I mean, when you let someone into your home, you expect —

MICHAEL. You *paid* me to come here! I get paid for dance lessons — not to share my personal life with you. And then you go calling around — I'll bet you checked on my marital status.

LILY. I did not! I just called all the veterinary hospitals in Seminole and asked if a Mrs. Minetti worked there.

MICHAE. *(Angrily)* Well stick a stogie in your mouth, dress you in drag, and call you J. Edgar Hoover! No job is worth this! Call Mr. Cunard, I don't care! Screw both of you! You can dance with each other!

(As he gathers his tote:)

LILY. If you lose this job don't blame anyone but yourself.

Between your dishonesty and your bad temper —

MICHAEL. *(Storming toward door.)* Only my ass can hear you now!

LILY. And your foul mouth! You act like a crazy man!

(MICHAEL turns at the door and musters his dignity.)

MICHAEL. I'm not crazy, I'm Italian! This is normal behavior for us. What's your excuse, Lily, for treating people badly?

(LILY looks at him a moment, suddenly timid and very vulnerable. She shrugs her shoulders and shakes her head.)

LILY. Menopause? *(MICHAEL has to smile.)* When you've lived as long as I have, you have so many scars from so many emotional wounds, you spend all your time running your fingers over them — and expecting new ones.

MICHAEL. Lily, if I were going to murder you, believe me, I would have done it during the first lesson.

LILY. Lying is a crime, too, Michael.

MICHAEL. You were calling my boss. I would have lost, not just this job, but every one after it.

LILY. But such an elaborate lie — the Seminole Cat, Dog —

MICHAEL. Bird and snake! Alright already! You kept asking me questions! I had to make stuff up to stay consistent.

LILY. But you started lying before I picked up the phone. You said you and your wife lived in Clearwater.

MICHAEL. You *assumed* I had a wife. I simply let you.

LILY. Why, Michael?

MICHAEL. I didn't know you well enough to be honest with you. And what I did know made me cautious.

LILY. What did you know?

MICHAEL. That your husband is a Baptist minister.

LILY. And that made me...?

MICHAEL. Possibly intolerant?

LILY. Intolerant?

MICHAEL. Of gay people? Unmarried dance instructor? Yoo-hoo. I'm gay, Lily.

(Pause, as LILY absorbs this, then:)

LILY. My husband always says, hate the sin, not the sinner.

MICHAEL. Yes, the bigot's anthem.

LILY. You don't even know the man!

MICHAEL. I had to rely on deductive reasoning! I couldn't afford to make a mistake! My job was on the line —

LILY. Your job! Your job! Don't use your job as an excuse for deception!

MICHAEL. Easy for you to say, sitting up here in fixed-income-social security-Medicare-heaven-with-a-view drinking Ensure daiquiris all day!

LILY. That is an insult! Don't blame me because you're — what's the expression — in the *pantry!*

MICHAEL. In the *closet!* And I'm not. I'm just careful about revealing my private life. This is the South, after all.

LILY. Well, *there's* a rationalization for you.

MICHAEL. Call it what you will. I'd rather be in the closet than in the coffin. I don't want some cracker in a pickup truck... Let's just say I have some scars, too, Lily — and they're not all "emotional."

LILY. Great choice, then — deciding to be a dance instructor in *Florida.*

MICHAEL. You think I wanted to end up living in the last

notch of the Bible Belt? It wasn't a choice. Some of us don't move here for the climate.

LILY. What do you mean?

MICHAEL. Nothing. That's my personal life. You know too much about me already. And what you know you learned by prying, not asking.

LILY. Oh...

MICHAEL. Look, Lily, I'm sorry, but maybe this just wasn't meant to be. I don't blame you...completely —

LILY. *(Indignant)* Well I should hope not! You're the one who —

MICHAEL. Okay! It's all my fault! I *lied* to you! But the real crime is, I lied about who I was to save my job. The money doesn't seem so important now.

(As MICHAEL turns to the door:)

LILY. That's not the way to punish yourself — or me. I mean, I don't want to be responsible for your losing your job.

MICHAEL. *(Turning back.)* Please, no charity. Besides, who really wants to take dance lessons from a passive-aggressive queen with a bad attitude?

LILY. Maybe a tight-assed, nosey old biddy.

(MICHAEL shakes his head, unconvinced.)

MICHAEL. I don't know...

LILY. Come on. You look so ridiculous standing there in your Zorro outfit. *(MICHAEL shrugs.)* And you *are* an excellent teacher, despite your —

MICHAEL. Insanity and dishonesty? Thank you.

LILY. *(Playfully)* Por nada.

MICHAEL. Exactly!

LILY. *(Suddenly impatient.)* Look, Michael, don't make me apologize, compliment you, *and* beg you in high-school Spanish. Stay or go. Either way, it's not going to make or ruin my day.

MICHAEL. In that case, I think I'll...go. *(And, with one last insolent look at LILY, MICHAEL exits without closing the door behind him. LILY stands startled for a moment, then sighs sadly and crosses to close the door. As she approaches it, MICHAEL jumps back into the room.)* Kidding! Got you again!

(LILY jumps back, startled, her hand to her chest.)

LILY. Good Lord you — ! Really, Michael, you don't do that to an old woman.

(As he begins setting up the CD player:)

MICHAEL. Oh, don't go all geriatric on me.

LILY. You made me go on about you, made me *humble* myself —

MICHAEL. I didn't make you.

LILY. You didn't stop me! It's all a game to you — toying with another soul.

MICHAEL. I wasn't "toying with another soul!" I was really upset. I just decided to forgive you very, very quickly. I'm not capable of holding a grudge.

LILY. I am.

MICHAEL. Okay, Lily, very Joan Crawford. But it's like dancing. Know when to change steps. Now, background: the Tango had it's origins in Argentina —

LILY. Just hold it, please! Normal people need transitions between events.

MICHAEL. Come on, Lily. Tick-tock. You don't want to look back on your deathbed and say, "Damn, I wish I hadn't wasted so much time on transitions!" *(As MICHAEL begins rolling up the carpet:)* The Tango is perhaps the most sensual, romantic of the Latin dances. It was created by the gaucho of Argentina, who, after a hard day on the pampas, got his much-needed R&R by picking up a floozie in the local taberna, getting her sloshed on cheap wine, then dragging her around the dance floor for a few measures before laying her.

(MICHAEL drags the carpet to the corner of the room and drops it.)

LILY. Is this background material standardized for the course or do you make it up as you go?

(MICHAEL places the vinyl footprints on the floor as:)

MICHAEL. I simply add honesty to it. The origin of all dancing is sexual, Lily — *(Seductively)* — a socially-acceptable way of feeling, smelling, attracting the beloved. But the Tango is the most direct expression. It is undiluted musical foreplay...*(Seductively, MICHAEL extends his hand to LILY, who hesitates for a moment. She then takes his hand and steps into the first footprint pattern. MICHAEL abruptly drops her hand — and his seductive manner — and crosses upstage to turn on the CD player. TANGO MUSIC* RISES.)* Now — the hold is closer, naturally, than in the other ballroom dances. And the dance, though dramatic, is fairly simple. Like sex, it's all in the execution. *(MICHAEL returns to LILY and takes her in his arms.)* Five steps in eight beats of music in 4/4 time, knees slightly flexed but firm, head poised, start with the right foot back for the *backward walk* — one and — releasing the left foot but letting the ball drag the floor slightly, sensually. That's it! Then lift that foot and place it behind — two and. Good! Right foot back — quick left to the side — then right toe closes to left with a weight shift. Perfect! Now *forward* on the left! Slow, slow, slow, quick, quick. Great! Back again!

(As LILY proficiently follows MICHAEL'S lead, the vinyl footprints are forgotten, and the dance flows gracefully until: The TELEPHONE RINGS. LILY stops.)

LILY. I'm sorry...
MICHAEL. No problem.

(LILY disengages from MICHAEL and answers the phone as he SHUTS THE MUSIC.)

LILY. *(Into receiver.)* Hello... *(With an exasperated look to MICHAEL.)* Yes, Ida.... Well, I don't know how, Ida, because I can barely hear it my myself. Is your ear trumpet nailed to the ceiling?! *(Getting angry.)* You know, Ida, I don't appreciate being compared to the dancing elephants in *Fantasia....* *(Suddenly smiling.)* No, I haven't seen the new version at the Imax Theater! Maybe the next time we're in Orlando.... I'd love to!.. Okay, then, 'bye!

(LILY hangs up and turns to MICHAEL, who seems confounded by the conversation.)

MICHAEL. Multiple personality?
LILY. No — it's perspective. At our age, who knows how much time we have left? Why waste it arguing?

MICHAEL. Never stopped me.

LILY. I noticed. But you can't understand yet.

MICHAEL. Think I can't understand mortality?

LILY. You're still enjoying the gift of youth, Michael. And, despite what my AARP newsletter claims, the world *does* belong to the young.

MICHAEL. No, it doesn't, Lily. We're renting it just like the rest of you.

(MICHAEL flicks on the CD player, and, as the TANGO TUNE* BEGINS again, he holds his arms open to LILY.)

MICHAEL. Tango, Señorita?

LILY. *(Smiling)* Encantada, Señor. *(She enters his hold and begins dancing effortlessly, then, in a Spanish accent:)* So how was your day on the pampas?

MICHAEL. *(Spanish accent.)* Well, Señorita, to be honest, my horse threw me, I have jock itch, and I'm very horny.

LILY. *(Spanish accent.)* Well don't get any ideas — you haven't even bought me a drink yet!

(As MICHAEL LAUGHS, LIGHTS DIM, leaving MICHAEL and LILY tangoing in silhouette before the SUNSET BACKDROP. As they dance OFF, TANGO MUSIC* FADES and the SUNSET EVOLVES TO NIGHT, THEN DAYBREAK, TO MIDDAY, then, as the voice of a soprano singing A VIENNESSE WALTZ TUNE* RISES, LIGHTS RISE on:)

---

*For information regarding music use, please see page 85

WEEK THREE — THE VIENNESE WALTZ

(As LIGHTS RISE, the DOORBELL RINGS and LILY rushes breath-lessly from the L hallway, trying to zip up the back of a rather frilly gown. WALTZ MUSIC* FADES as she crosses to the front door, calling:)

LILY. Michael?
MICHAEL. *(OS - German accent.)* No, it's your dance instructor, *Helmut.*

(LILY smiles and throws open the door to find MICHAEL dressed in a well-worn but still handsome tuxedo. He carries his usual tote.)

LILY. I knew you'd dress up for the Viennese Waltz! I did, too!
MICHAEL. *(Indicating the back of her gown.)* Well, almost —
LILY. I know. Sorry to subject you to an old woman's back, but would you mind zipping me up?

(Turning her back to him.)

MICHAEL. *(Zipping; German accent.)* Not at all. And your

back is as pretty as a strudel.

LILY. Yeah — pasty and flaky. *(She crosses to the kitchen, removes pastry from the refrigerator, and begins preparing instant coffee. MICHAEL removes the CD player and begins placing the vinyl footprints on the floor.)* You know my husband and I visited Vienna years ago — so beautiful. Schonbrunn Palace, the Lippizaner stallions, the Ring Strasse. We ate Sachertorte in the cafe where it was invented. And everyone was so nice.

MICHAEL. I'm sure. They're very hospitable people. They rolled out the red carpet for Hitler, too.

LILY. Oh, good Lord, don't blame the whole country. Have you ever been there?

MICHAEL. No. I was tempted to take the Nazi atrocity tour of Europe, starting in the country where it all began — Austria — but I decided it would be a little depressing.

LILY. *You're* a little depressing. That was half a century ago Michael. Get over it.

MICHAEL. I'd love to, but you have to keep your guard up. Those people are still around — baiting Jews, blacks, gays, anyone who's different. And you're right — they're not just Austrian or German. They could be anybody. Anybody you pass on the street.

LILY. *(Crossing to coffee table with cups and saucers.)* What a negative way to view the world.

MICHAEL. Sorry. Your rose-colored goggles get knocked off pretty quickly when you're swimming against the mainstream.

LILY. I'm aware of prejudice and injustice, too, Michael —

MICHAEL. Only vicariously, Lily. If the world belongs to anyone, it belongs to straight white people.

LILY. My God, Michael, what happened to you?

MICHAEL. You've heard of the angry young man? I'm the angry middle-aged man.

LILY. I didn't learn much as a minister's wife, but I remember Matthew 5:44: "Bless them that curse you, do good to them that hate you and persecute you."

MICHAEL. And make sure you have Blue Cross.

LILY. You hate too easily.

MICHAEL. It's inevitable when you think everyone hates you.

LILY. That will consume you.

MICHAEL. That's what I thought until I was twenty-five and I realized that, no matter how loving I was, there would always be some big fat bigot trying to make my life miserable. Speaking of which, where's your husband today?

LILY. Are you insinuating that my husband is a bigot?

MICHAEL. Let's see...Southern Baptist minister from South Carolina.

LILY. You don't know how he feels —

MICHAEL. How could I? He's never here. But I would guess your husband is the guy who always knows who has a drop of black blood, or whose name is Jewish, or who's screwing who —

LILY. How dare you — !

MICHAEL. What?! Maybe if he were here he could contradict me.

LILY. Why should he?!

MICHAEL. *Could* he, is the question. He's always conveniently absent when I arrive.

LILY. *(Defensive)* He doesn't want to interrupt my lessons.

MICHAEL. How thoughtful. Where does he go?

LILY. Why he...walks on the beach, spends time with friends, goes to the mall.

MICHAEL. *(Game show host.)* Beach, friends, mall! Is that your final answer?

LILY. Michael, I don't know if you had too much sugar or caffeine with lunch or what, but maybe we should reschedule this lesson for tomorrow, when, hopefully, your brain chemistry will have normalized!

MICHAEL. Fat chance. I got all dressed up in my ratty tuxedo to give you this lesson —

LILY. Well I don't want it!

(LILY begins clearing items from the coffee table and returning them to the kitchen.)

MICHAEL. And you put on your fuck-me dress!

(LILY stops and turns, livid.)

LILY. Get out!

MICHAEL. No, I have no intention of driving my ass all the way back here to Sun City tomorrow!

(MICHAEL moves to plug in the CD player.)

LILY. Don't you plug that in! *(MICHAEL looks at LILY defiantly for a moment, then deliberately inserts the plug into the wall socket.)* You annoying, recalcitrant reprobate!

MICHAEL. Wow, thanks, I'm not used to such high-class insults. A simple "crazy faggot" would have sufficed. Now, *background:* when the Waltz was introduced it was considered scandalous—

LILY. *(Crossing to the door and throwing it open.)* I told you to go!

MICHAEL. Look, I know women of your generation are used to having men do everything they demand, but I'm not a man of your generation!

LILY. Why you're not even a —

MICHAEL. There it is! Go ahead!

LILY. A gentleman.

MICHAEL. Nice save. So I was saying, the Waltz was a scandal because for the first time a man and woman danced embracing each other —

LILY. Should I call the dance studio —

MICHAEL. Oh, no! Don't let Mr. Cunard hit me with the big paddle he uses on the bad dancing boys!

LILY. Or the police?!

MICHAEL. Why not just call your imaginary husband?!

LILY. What?!

MICHAEL. You don't have a husband, Lily! He died six years ago!

LILY. *(Slamming door.)* Hush! The neighbors will hear you!

MICHAEL. Who do you think told me?

LILY. Who?

MICHAEL. First, somebody at the dance studio, but I told him he was mistaken. How could virtuous Mrs. Harrison, our paragon of honesty —

LILY. Oh, get off your soapbox and spit it out! Who told you?

MICHAEL. Some old codger cornered me in the elevator on the way up and told me your life story. He would have shown me the video of your husband's funeral, if he'd had it.

LILY. *(Bitterly)* Mr. Crumwald. That meddlesome old fart.

MICHAEL. My God, Lily, an imaginary husband.

LILY. You had an imaginary wife!

MICHAEL. Just for a few minutes. You had yours for six years!

LILY. At least mine existed at one time.

MICHAEL. That's even weirder. You know, in the craziness sweepstakes, first I thought I was running way ahead of you, then I thought we finished nose and nose, but here you are in the winner's circle with a floral horseshoe around your neck!

(LILY crosses to the couch and sits, defeated.)

LILY. You have no idea what it's like for a woman alone.

MICHAEL. Is this the part where you try to arouse my sympathy in order to excuse your behavior?

LILY. No, how can I ask you to excuse me after I —

MICHAEL. Excoriated me mercilessly — just last week! — for doing exactly the same thing! I mean, you elevated the double standard to new heights, then crowned it with self-righteousness! How *could* you, Lily?

LILY. You're right. How could I?

MICHAEL. Oh, don't try squirming out of this by accepting blame! You deserve to spend a few minutes writhing in pathetic self defense.

LILY. I have no defense.

MICHAEL. No defense is no defense!

LILY. But I do have a reason.

MICHAEL. *(Taking a seat.)* Okay. Roll it out so I can kick it around. But I'm warning you, although I've never dated women, I had a mother. So I've been inoculated against gender blackmail.

LILY. After Harlan died, I found myself saying things like "My husband and I..." or "I'll have to ask my husband." At first it was inadvertent, but then it became intentional. I just couldn't give him up.

MICHAEL. Why not freeze dry him and perch him in his favorite chair?

LILY. How insensitive!

MICHAEL. I warned you this spit wouldn't fly! But keep trying, if you want.

LILY. Later, I admitted to myself that it was more than refusing to part with my husband; I didn't want to give up the mantle of protection that having a husband affords a woman. People start to disappear when they get older. Did you know that?

MICHAEL. I knew they shrank a little bit.

(LILY shoots him a look.)

LILY. Anyway, you start to disappear. The hostess at Howard Johnson's looks right through you, store clerks talk over your head. With someone holding onto your hand, you feel that you just might hang on to all three dimensions. But an old woman, without a husband, becomes completely invisible.

(MICHAEL is moved, but is reluctant to show it.)

MICHAEL. Oh, God, Lily.

(Knowing she is scoring, LILY continues:)

LILY. So you can imagine how vulnerable I felt having a stranger in my home. You might try to rip me off, or even rape me — *(She and MICHAEL share a look.)* I guess rape was out.

MICHAEL. *(Nodding)* Yeah...

LILY. But who knew? So if you, or the delivery boy, or the repair man thought Harlan was coming home, he could still protect me. Like, if you don't have a watch dog, having one of those tapes with a dog barking on it.

MICHAEL. Those don't fool anybody, and neither do fictitious husbands after a while.

LILY. I know. I knew I couldn't keep it up for six weeks, but I thought that once I felt I could trust you —

MICHAEL. You would tell me something that would make me *dis*trust you.

LILY. Okay! So I didn't think it through! But when you *lied* to me —

MICHAEL. *The same lie* — ironically enough!

LILY. YES, MICHAEL — IRONICALLY ENOUGH! Of course, getting a   dance instructor with sociopathic tendencies didn't help to allay my fears.

MICHAEL. Hey!

LILY. *(Quickly)* But, regardless, I was too hard on you, and I apologize. Most of the anger I vented at you was really directed at myself.... Well, some of it, anyway.

MICHAEL. Before you qualify your apology completely, I accept it. And...I'm sorry I was so obnoxious when I came in. I felt, you know —

LILY. I know. Thank you, Michael.

MICHAEL. And I want to tell you...

LILY. Yes?

(MICHAEL takes LILY'S hands and looks directly into her eyes.)

MICHAEL. I see you, Lily — in all three dimensions. You're right here.

LILY. *(Moved)* Thank you.

(MICHAEL rises and turns on the CD   player. WALTZ TUNE*
RISES as MICHAEL turns to LILY and bows.)

---

*For information regarding music use, please see page 85

MICHAEL. May I have this dance?
LILY. Delighted.

(As MICHAEL clasps LILY.)

MICHAEL. Waltz music is in three-four time, meaning three beats per measure —
LILY. Can we just dance now, Michael? You can tell me later.
MICHAEL. Of course...

(As MICHAEL begins moving LILY around the floor, she follows gracefully until:
The PHONE RINGS.)

MICHAEL. Should we ignore that?
LILY. If we do, she'll probably dial 911. *(LILY crosses to the phone and picks up the receiver as MICHAEL SHUTS THE MUSIC.)* Hello.... Well, ratchet down the volume control on your hearing aid, Ida! You're not supposed to hear better than Superman!... So go ahead! Complain to the board, you old kill joy! I'm wearing my fuck-me dress and I'm going to dance!

(LILY slams down the receiver. MICHAEL stares at her in wonder.)

MICHAEL. I think you've been spending way too much time with me.
LILY. Oh, really! The nerve of that woman! She thinks she's the Dean of Girls. *(Then, uneasily)* You think I was too hard on her? Maybe I should call her back.
MICHAEL. Don't worry; she'll call you.

(MICHAEL TURNS ON THE MUSIC again.)

MICHAEL. You don't really need an instructor for the Waltz, do you, Lily?

LILY. No... *(Opening her arms to MICHAEL.)* But I do need a partner.

(MICHAEL takes LILY in a hold and begins an intricate pattern of steps with her as FOREGROUND LIGHTS FADE. The two dance in silhouette before the lighted backdrop, then dance off. WALTZ MUSIC FADES as BACKDROP CHANGES FROM SUNSET TO NIGHT, TO SUNRISE, and:)

WEEK FOUR — THE FOXTROT

(BACKDROP CONTINUES CHANGING FROM SUNRISE TO MIDDAY as a bright FOXTROT TUNE* RISES. FOREGROUND LIGHTS RISE, revealing that the carpet and furniture are not configured for a dance lesson.
The DOORBELL RINGS. LILY does not appear. The DOORBELL RINGS AGAIN. LILY enters from the L hallway. She wears a dowdy robe and slippers and appears far from ready for company. She crosses to the door and peeps through the hole. MUSIC FADES OUT as:)

MICHAEL. *(OS)* You know, I think they put that thing on backwards, because I can see your big fish eye.

LILY. Michael? Didn't the dance studio call you?

MICHAEL. *(OS)* No. Do I get to come in?

LILY. I'm a little under the weather today. I called and canceled.

MICHAEL. *(OS)* Do you have a man in there?!

LILY. I'm not properly dressed to receive guests.

MICHAEL. *(OS)* Oh, don't get all Jane Austin about it. Just open the door. I can take it. *(LILY opens the door with a sigh. MICHAEL bursts impatiently into the room. He wears a snazzy coat and tie and a fedora and carries his tote.)* Finally! *(Focusing on LILY.)* My God, you really *aren't* dressed to receive guests. Was that your husband's robe?

LILY. I told you — ! Oh, hell, I'll change.

(As she crosses to the L hallway, MICHAEL calls after her:)

MICHAEL. Think Foxtrot!

(LILY throws him a dubious look before exiting L.)

MICHAEL. *(To himself.)* Good, it worked.
LILY. *(OS)* What?!

(MICHAEL begins rolling up the carpet and pushing back the furniture.)

MICHAEL. *(Calling to her.)* I said, when I worked on Broadway —
LILY. *(OS)* You were on Broadway?
MICHAEL. Yes. I was a chorus boy. A good one, too. Did you see *A Chorus Line?*
LILY. *(OS)* Yes!
MICHAEL. Well, I wasn't in it. But it was the story of my life. I worked constantly.
LILY. *(OS)* So what happened?
MICHAEL. Are you implying that my present hasn't lived up to my past?
LILY. *(OS)* No, I —
MICHAEL. I mean, isn't it a natural progression for a Broadway chorus boy to become a dance instructor in Heaven's

Boot Camp?

LILY. *(OS)* Well, that's a nice thing to say to an old woman.

MICHAEL. Oh, don't get so proprietary about death, Lily. We're all waiting in line for the inevitable. Who knows whose turn will come first?

LILY. *(OS)* If that's your way of cheering up a sick person, call Dale Carnegie.

MICHAEL. I'm a dancer, not a social worker. So, I was saying, when I was dancing professionally, illness was not an excuse for missing a performance.

LILY. *(OS)* How many sixty-eight year old chorus dancers did you know?

MICHAEL. Can't wait 'till *I'm* old so I can use *my* age as an excuse for everything.

(LILY enters L, completely transformed in heels, make-up, and a smart black-and-white cocktail dress.)

LILY. And you will.

MICHAEL. Look at you! Dressed for cocktails at the Stork Club.

LILY. Oh, stop. It's all smoke and mirrors. I still don't feel well enough to —

MICHAEL. Yes, you do! You dressed to foxtrot!

LILY. I did not!

MICHAEL. Yes, you did! That's a little foxtrot dress if ever I saw one! And Cuban heels, you seductive slut!

LILY. Michael!

(MICHAEL ignores her indignation and pulls a small bag from his tote.)

MICHAEL. Oh, here. I had this delicious soup at lunch and got some take-out for you.

LILY. No thanks, I — what kind?

MICHAEL. Cream of potato.

LILY. Maybe I'll have just a taste —

(The PHONE RINGS. MICHAEL turns to LILY in surprise.)

MICHAEL. We haven't even put on the music yet!

(As LILY crosses to the phone, MICHAEL begins opening the take-out container at the kitchen counter.)

LILY. That's not Ida. *(Lifting receiver.)* Hello.... Yes.... Oh, but he's right — *(She stops, looks at MICHAEL, then speaks into receiver again.)* Friday might work. Can I get back to you?... Thank you *(She hangs up receiver and crosses to the bar.)* That was the dance studio.

MICHAEL. Oh?

LILY. Yes, they were calling to reschedule the lesson. They told me they'd spoken to you, and you said you were free Friday.

MICHAEL. I thought they were talking about your *next* lesson.

LILY. They told you I was sick, didn't they?!

MICHAEL. No, I don't think they mentioned it.

LILY. That's why you brought the *soup*, isn't it?!

MICHAEL. *(Exploding)* Good Lord, Lily, do you have to examine everything under your neutron microscope? I brought you some goddamn soup!

LILY. Don't curse at me! I'm touched!

MICHAEL. You don't sound touched!

LILY. I just don't know why you have to lie about doing something nice!

MICHAEL. I don't know why you have to question every-thing! I was a little concerned about you, okay!?

LILY. So why rush over to resume our usual pattern of lying and arguing?!

MICHAEL. Because that's what we do! Every relationship has a foundation. That's ours!

LILY. Oh.... That's very nice, Michael. Thank you.

MICHAEL. Oh shut up —

LILY. You have an unusual bedside manner.

MICHAEL. — now that you've made me miserable.

LILY. Don't be petulant. *(Taking a sip of soup.)* Ummm. Delicious!

MICHAEL. *(Suddenly cheerful.)* Isn't it? *(As LILY reaches for another spoonful:)* No, get off your perch and come sit on the sofa like a lady. *(As they cross to the sofa:)* I get it in this little shop in Madeira Beach.

(LILY sits and takes another sip of soup as MICHAEL sits beside her)

LILY. I love it. It tastes like my mother's. She was a great cook.

MICHAEL. So was mine.

LILY. Does she still? I mean, is she —

MICHAEL. She died last year.

LILY. Oh, I'm sorry. That's so recent.

MICHAEL. Feels that way. Thanks. She was sick for a few years.

LILY. With what...may I ask?

MICHAEL. Sure — Alzheimer's.

LILY. Oh, how terrible. She lived here?

MICHAEL. Yes. In Clearwater. The house I live in now. The house I grew up in. She died there.

LILY. And you took care of her?

MICHAEL. Yeah. That's why I moved from New York. I was talking to her on the phone one day, and she told me that my father was at the Winn Dixie buying a Thanksgiving turkey. Well, it was February, and my father had been dead for five years, so I flew down right away and took her to the doctor. Diagnosis of advanced Alzheimer's. I emptied my apartment in New York and moved down here.

LILY. Any siblings to help you?

MICHAEL. Only child — surprise!

(LILY smiles.)

LILY. She was very lucky to have you.

MICHAEL. Oh, I was the lucky one. She kept me centered, taught me humanity. She had a calming effect on me. Guess you can tell she's gone.

LILY. And you looked after her all by yourself?

MICHAEL. I couldn't afford nursing care. And I couldn't put her in a home.

LILY. My God, Michael, that must have been punishing.

MICHAEL. Not really. You just have to change your priorities. I knew her time was slipping away, so our time together became more precious. There were blessings: she always recognized me, always knew my name to the end. I'd walk into her room, see her looking around completely confused, disoriented, not recognizing one of the mementos that chronicled her life, and I would stand in her line of vision and she would suddenly smile and say my name.

(LILY puts a comforting hand on MICHAEL'S shoulder.)

LILY. Michael...

MICHAEL. I was her only point of reference, her final solid landmark in a sea of detached objects and floating mysteries.

LILY. What a good son you were.

(MICHAEL shrugs and rises.)

MICHAEL. Nah.

LILY. You gave up your career in New York to look after your mother.

MICHAEL. Not much of a career anymore. I was getting a little long in the tooth for a chorus boy, and the word "difficult" was beginning to appear in invisible ink on my resume.

LILY. Why was that?

MICHAEL. Do you have to ask?

LILY. Well, yes. I know you weren't born this way.

MICHAEL. Let's just say my life off stage was getting a lot less enchanting than life on. Want to dance?

LILY. No, Michael, I really don't feel well —

MICHAEL. What kind of deceptive disease is this, anyway, that leaves you looking healthy and vibrant?

LILY. What leaves me looking healthy and vibrant is Max Factor. The disease is a kind of, I don't know — malaise.

MICHAEL. Malaise? Did you find that in the Southern Belle Medical Dictionary along with "the vapors"?

LILY. Laugh. When you're seventy-two —

(LILY stops. MICHAEL smiles at her revealed deception.)

MICHAEL. Maybe this *is* a serious disease if it causes you to age four years in one day.

LILY. *(Chagrinned)* If you say your real age out loud, your face hears you.

MICHAEL. Look, either way you're not Miss Teenage America. As if I care.

LILY. *(Suddenly flaring.)* Of course *you* don't care! It's *my* vanity! And if you weren't badgering me to death I wouldn't go betraying myself like that!

(LILY storms into the kitchen.)

MICHAEL. Look, don't blame *me* because you spilled the beans all over yourself.

LILY. You know, Michael, I only got dressed because you were pissing me off —

MICHAEL. Good thing your imaginary husband didn't hear that!

LILY. *(Continuing)* And, frankly, it gave me a chance to get out of the room before you *annoyed* me to death. In fact, did they check your mother's death certificate? Maybe that's what she *really* died of....*(MICHAEL stands stunned. LILY is immediately remorseful.)* Oh, Michael, if I could take those words back —

MICHAEL. Oh, I know. Believe me. I've wished that so many times myself — as you can imagine. Want to snatch them right out of the air. But you can't.

LILY. I know, but I'm so sorry. I didn't mean —

MICHAEL. No, you *did* mean it. You just didn't mean to say it.

LILY. No, I *didn't* mean it. It's just, when I don't feel well, I strike out.

MICHAEL. I can relate to *that,* too. In fact, you know how they say you see your life flash before your eyes before you die and you regret every lousy thing you've ever said or done?

LILY. Uh-huh.

MICHAEL. Well, I do that every day. But there are limits, Lily. You crossed a line. *(MICHAEL crosses to his tote as if to snatch it up and exit. Instead, he removes the CD player.)* But I cross them all the time. That's why I can't hold a grudge.

(MICHAEL crosses to the wall and plugs in the CD player.)

LILY. It's just that when you're alone, with no one to talk to, you forget the rules of polite discourse.

MICHAEL. I never even *learned* them myself.

LILY. *(Continuing)* And words tumble right out of your mouth.

MICHAEL. Like now. I forgave you five minutes ago. Shut up already.

(MICHAEL presses the PLAY button on the CD player, sending the FOXTROT TUNE* into the room. He then takes the vinyl foot-steps from his tote and tosses them in a pattern on the floor. LILY crosses to the CD player and SHUTS IT.)

LILY. No, I don't want you harboring some unspoken resentment against me.

MICHAEL. Okay — I hate you! Feel better? *(He crosses to the CD player and flicks it ON. Holds open his arms.)* Want to dance?

LILY. I don't suppose I could refuse now.

MICHAEL. Gender blackmail is a two-way street. *(LILY enters MICHAEL'S hold as:)* Now the Social Foxtrot was intro-

*For information regarding music use, please see page 85

duced by Vernon Castle and quickly became the popular musical excuse for pressing your groin against that of someone you admired without getting arrested.

LILY. Michael, really, you take all the charm out of it.

MICHAEL. Oh, think back, Lily! That *is* the charm!

LILY. Not in South Carolina.

MICHAEL. *(Southern accent.)* Oh, don't try that Miss Mellie routine on me. I can just see you in the tobacco shed with your hoop skirt over your head.

(MICHAEL mimes lifting a hoop skirt over his head.)

LILY. Michael!

MICHAEL. Now, the Foxtrot. The basic steps in the follow position are — *(LILY follows easily as he moves her over the vinyl footprints with:)* Right foot back, slow. Left foot back, slow. Right foot to side, quick. Left foot closing to right, quick. Right foot forward, slow. Left foot forward, slow. Right foot to side, quick. Left foot closing to right, quick. Now in time to the music and off the footprints. *(LILY follows smoothly without a misstep.)* That's it! Beautiful! I'm wasting my time and you're wasting your money! Now *promenade walk* and *chasse!*

(They do, and the PHONE RINGS. As if by rote, they stop, LILY crosses to the phone, MICHAEL crosses to the CD player and SHUTS IT.)

LILY. I knew the promenade walk and chasse would get her.

MICHAEL. Always a show stopper.

LILY. *(Picking up receiver.)* Hello, Ida.... No, the Busch Gardens Clydesdales are not giving a command performance in my living room....*(With a glance at MICHAEL.)* No, he's a normal-sized man....

MICHAEL. Thanks, Babe.

LILY. And that's about it for normal.... *(MICHAEL shoots her a look.)* Ida, you have gone from presumptuous to downright rude.... No, I may not go to Epcot. I'm not sure I want to get stuck on the bus sitting next to some nosey old busybody!

(She slams down the receiver.)

MICHAEL. Ooo — Gray Panther cat fight.

LILY. Well, she makes me so mad!

MICHAEL. Yeah, you ought to go down there and kick her ass!

LILY. (Suddenly fretful.) Oh, maybe I was too hard on her.

MICHAEL. And on to remorse with *no transition.*

LILY. I'll sit next to her on the bus to Orlando to make amends.

MICHAEL. I hate to interrupt your orgy of self recrimination, but tell me something.

LILY. Yes?

MICHAEL. At the risk of committing career suicide, you really don't need these lessons, do you?

LILY. Oh, I don't know —

MICHAEL. I mean, you do these dances as well as I do.

LILY. Well, once you refresh my memory, some of it *does* come back to me.

MICHAEL. A *lot.* Lily, you're Irene Castle, Isadora Duncan, Marge *and* Gower Champion.

LILY. Not really. And I haven't had much experience with the Cha Cha or the Contemporary Dance.

MICHAEL. They're hardly worth the price of the course.

LILY. And then there's all your interesting background information.

MICHAEL. Lily, you're a pro. You've probably taken other

classes, haven't you?

LILY. Maybe a few. But nothing like this, in my own home. I hated going to the dance studios and hanging around with a bunch of old widows waiting for my turn in a group class. Seeing the look of pity on the face of the young receptionist. It took all the magic out of it.

MICHAEL. Social anxiety disorder — I saw it in a commercial. There's a drug for that.

LILY. I know — *youth!*

MICHAEL. No, you're just spending too much time alone. Believe me, I know. Why not go to a dance? Meet some nice men your age?

LILY. *(Smiling ruefully.)* Do you have any idea what most men my age are like? First, they're usually married or already dead. And the few available survivors are, one, less than attentive to anything not involving food, and, two, I don't know what they're eating but they all seem to share a certain proclivity for the production of gas.

MICHAEL. Thanks, that gives me a lot to look forward to.

LILY. Well it may be your destiny, but it's my reality.

MICHAEL. Well...why don't you go dancing with me?

LILY. Oh, you have better things to do with your evenings than drag an old —

MICHAEL. Self-deprecating woman to a dance. There's one at Gulfport next Thursday. We could go there instead of having our usual lesson.

LILY. I don't know —

MICHAEL. Why not? Share your talent with someone besides me — *(Stomps on floor.)* — and Ida.

(LILY considers for just a moment before agreeing happily.)

LILY. Okay...

MICHAEL. It's a date, then. I'll pick you up at seven sharp.

LILY. Seven sharp. It's...a date. It's been so long since I've had one, I can barely say it.

MICHAEL. Get used to it, Babe, because — *(MICHAEL crosses to the CD player, and TURNS IT ON.)* The best is yet to come!

(MICHAEL strides to LILY and — affectionately — takes her in his arms. As they begin to dance, LILY closes her eyes, and: FOREGROUND LIGHTS DIM slowly leaving MICHAEL and LILY dancing in silhouette before the LIGHTED BACKDROP, which CHANGES FROM AFTERNOON, to SUNSET, to EVENING. As LILY and MICHAEL continue dancing, LIGHTS DIM TO BLACKOUT, and:)

ACT BREAK

WEEK FIVE — THE CHA-CHA

(The LIGHTED BACKDROP REMAINS AT EVENING as CHA-CHA TUNE* RISES. Then FOREGROUND LIGHTS RISE and laughter is audible outside the front door. The sound of a key entering the lock, and the door opens. MICHAEL and LILY burst into the room, laughing. LILY wears a lovely evening dress and is artfully made-up and coifed. MICHAEL wears black tie with a dinner jacket.

LILY shushes MICHAEL as she closes the door behind him and turns on a few LIGHTS. Furniture and carpet are in non-dance-lesson configuration. CHA-CHA MUSIC FADES OUT as:)

LILY. Shh — we'll wake the neighbors.

MICHAEL. It's only nine-thirty...oh, I forgot, that's midnight in over-seventy time.

LILY. Exactly. How about some decaf?

MICHAEL. Okay. *(As LILY crosses to the kitchen:)* Did you get a load of that flaming queen?

LILY. *(Preparing coffee.)* Which one? The place was crawling with them.

MICHAEL. Present company included. The one dancing with

---

the woman who looked like Mother Time.

LILY. No shortage of those, either.

MICHAEL. He had black Spandex pants —

LILY. Sequined lapels?

MICHAEL. Yeah. Boy, he made me look butch. In fact, he made *you* look butch. What a showboat! Although those pants *showed* a little more than he wanted to.

LILY. Actually — a little less.

MICHAEL. *(Amused and astonished.)* My God, Lily, you're becoming a bigger bitch than I am.

LILY. Don't try to take credit for it. I had natural talent, which I had to squelch for years as a minister's wife. Such a relief to be able to violate a few commandments before it's too late.

MICHAEL. Somehow I can't picture that.

LILY. What?

MICHAEL. You as a minister's wife.

LILY. Picture me biting my tongue a lot, smiling insincerely, and looking pious. Hell, it was a job. All jobs require a certain sacrifice, a certain attitude, even a certain uniform — print dresses in my case.

MICHAEL. How'd you do it?

LILY. It wasn't so bad at first, just after Harlan and I were married. At the beginning of our relationship I felt expanded by our love; toward the end I felt diminished by it.

MICHAEL. But you stayed with him.

(LILY serves coffee in the living room. Both sit at the coffee table.)

LILY. Harlan was essentially a good man, but even a spouse wears on you after a while.

MICHAEL That's what happens when you marry outside your

gender.

LILY. Sometimes it's necessity and inertia that hold a marriage together, not love.

MICHAEL. What about children?

LILY. We had one girl — Nan. She died when she was twenty.

MICHAEL. Oh. I'm so sorry.

LILY. Thank you. *(Then, quickly.)* It didn't bring Harlan and me any closer together. That's why I got my degree and started teaching. I had always had a passion for literature, so I decided to turn my passion into my profession. It saved my sanity.

MICHAEL. Lily, I had no idea...

LILY. You didn't think I'd been hanging around for seventy-two years waiting for life to happen to me, did you?

MICHAEL. No, I mean, I've always accused people of pre-judging me, and I did the same with you — and your husband.

LILY. Well, you missed me by a mile, but, I must admit, you came pretty close with Harlan. That's why I don't defend him too vigorously when you attack him. At first I was charmed by the way he could quote a piece of Scripture to suit any occasion. Then I realized it was a substitute for *original thinking.* In his zeal to live according to the letter of God's law, he lost his humanity between the lines. He could be very close-minded, very cruel, almost... And you were right; he didn't, you know, he didn't like...gays. *(MICHAEL nods. They both sip their coffee in silence for a moment.)* I told myself early in the marriage not to expect from him what I gave to him. But later, I asked myself how he could give back so little.... Still, I must say, our relationship has improved since he died. *(MICHAEL laughs.)* No, I mean, I've learned to understand him and forgive him. Relationships do continue after death, you know.

MICHAEL. However unilaterally.

LILY. Yes — however. They *have* to evolve for the survivor — or you go mad locked in a time capsule, reliving the same moments over and over.

MICHAEL. Believe me — I know.

LILY. Your mother?

MICHAEL. No, I was thinking of a friend of mine who died years ago. *(Before LILY can respond.)* So how was your trip to Epcot?

LILY. Well, a little tiring, but fun. It's reassuring to visit a safe little world with a gate and walls to keep reality at bay.

MICHAEL. Safe — and conveniently concentrated! I mean, a simple three-minute walk takes you from the Pyramid of the Sun in Mexico to the Doge's Palace in Venice.

LILY. I know! The money saved on air travel alone more than compensates for the price of admission.

MICHAEL. *(Smiling)* Did you and Ida bury the hatchet?

LILY. No! I didn't see her. I should give her a call. I hope she didn't boycott the trip on my account.

MICHAEL. I doubt it. So you didn't have a lunch companion in Morocco?

LILY. No, I sat by myself.

MICHAEL. No other friends on the trip?

LILY. Some other people from the building, but I'm not much of a mixer. Do you ever get the feeling that you're just passing through life — watching it go by like a passenger at a train window — never really touching it, never really becoming engaged by it?

MICHAEL. No, but that's my goal.

LILY. You don't mean that. That feeling of detachment — secure but isolated — for the last few years I've been spending more and more of my life that way.

MICHAEL. You have to extend yourself, Lily.

LILY. I did — I met you.

MICHAEL. You *hired* me.

LILY. So I'm an old woman with a little money to spend on companionship. So what?

MICHAEL. So nothing. I'm just saying there are other ways to meet people. Buying them can get expensive.

LILY. If you have to shame me to preserve your pride, go ahead.

MICHAEL. I'm not! I don't think there's anything wrong with paying for company. For God's sake, I've paid for...company.

LILY. You mean...sex?

MICHAEL. If you want to call it that.

LILY. You've *paid* for *sex?*

MICHAEL. Lily, one way or another, you *always* pay for sex. But, yes, I've paid with cash.

LILY. Why, Michael? You're a handsome man.

MICHAEL. Same reason you paid for companionship — convenience and availability.

LILY. But you're young — why not go out and meet someone nice?

MICHAEL. Where? A smokey bar? A men's room? The Gulf Coast isn't quite set up yet for meaningful gay encounters. Besides, I'm always afraid of running into one of those crazy rednecks from *Deliverance.*

LILY. Oh, that's just an excuse. People who are alone are that way for one of two reasons: either they *want* to be alone, or everyone else thinks they *should* be.

MICHAEL. I attest to the former and confess to the latter.

LILY. At your age you should be looking for romance.

MICHAEL. That's just a fifties word for sex.

LILY. Love, then.

MICHAEL. Three months of ecstasy and a lifetime of agony.

LILY. You're cynical now, but you'll find someone, and then —

MICHAEL. Don't curse me. I'm hoping my luck will hold out.

LILY. How badly could you have suffered to end up so jaded?

MICHAEL. Let's see.... Should we start in New York, or just do Florida?

(LILY considers for a moment, then:)

LILY. *(Eagerly)* New York.

MICHAEL. No, let's skip New York. That's another level of misery entirely. But my Florida encounters have a grotesque charm about them — like those stuffed baby alligators you find in the curio shops.

LILY. You don't have to —

MICHAEL. No, I want to — just to prove I've given it the old college try. And, speaking of which, let's start with the University of South Florida student, a very handsome young man who transported me to a place I'd never been before.

LILY. Really?

MICHAEL. Yes — *Hell.* After going out with me a few times, he decided he wasn't gay. And to prove it, he decided to knock me around a little bit. At a most inopportune moment, I might add.

LILY. Oh, Michael, were you hurt?

MICHAEL. I got in a few good licks and got out with all my appendages attached, so I consider myself lucky. Then there was the married man —

LILY. Married?

MICHAEL. Yes — to a *woman.* We were like that yogurt —

you know, fruit on the bottom?

LILY. What...? Oh... OH!

MICHAEL. So anyway — that was obviously doomed. A relationship based purely on..."romance."

LILY. Didn't you meet anyone you felt...deeper feelings for?

MICHAEL. "Deeper feelings?" Do you mean "love?"

LILY. Well I didn't want to set you off again.

MICHAEL. No, you can't say it for the same reason I can't. You know it's the ultimate essential lie, society's great myth -- Santa Claus for adults.

LILY. I don't think that.

MICHAEL. Then you're still a victim of mass hypnosis. But, yes, I did delude myself into believing I felt that *thing* for someone.

LILY. Where did you meet him?

MICHAEL. The gay-and-lesbian-books section at Barnes & Noble. I was trying to make contact by flashing around Larry Kramer's *Faggots*.... That's a book, not a Vegas revue.

LILY. Oh.

MICHAEL. And he was reading some gay personal grooming book — *Sprucing Up Bruce*, or something like that. As if he needed any help at becoming a better man trap. He had one of those magical faces — dark hair, blue eyes, perfect mouth — a face you wanted to kiss or just keep talking to — anything to stay engaged, connected to it. Even after I'd seen that perfect mouth snarl and yell obscenities at me, I wanted to stay connected to it.

LILY. So how did it end?

MICHAEL. How does it always end for the more caring person in a relationship — abject humiliation and depression. I kept trying to convince myself that he would improve, become kinder. But beautiful people, I discovered, can get through life without practicing any social skills. I finally had to admit that he would never change — and I told him so.

LILY. Well, at least you had the satisfaction of telling him!

MICHAEL. Yes — right after he pushed me out the door of his Mustang.

LILY. Oh, Michael — !

MICHAEL. Don't worry; he was only doing about five miles an hour at the time.

LILY. Were you injured?

MICHAEL. I'd like to say he only bruised my pride, but some soft tissue was involved, too.

LILY. You should have had him arrested!

MICHAEL. And become an object of ridicule and mirth in the local paper? No thanks. Besides, you can't count on Mr. Policeman to be solicitous to victims of gay domestic violence.

LILY. I see.... How terrible.

MICHAEL. Yeah, well.

LILY. So that was it? You gave up after that?

MICHAEL. My God, Lily, have you been listening?!

LILY. It wasn't *all* bad, was it?

MICHAEL. How much abuse would you like me to endure?

LILY. Well, I mean, you had some fun. You got out.

(MICHAEL shoots LILY a stern look.)

MICHAEL. So did Abraham Lincoln.

LILY. You want me to tell you it's okay to give up, but it's not, Michael.

MICHAEL. Look, I don't need any of your Mr. Rogers-little-engine-that-could tips on human relations. *(Setting down his cup.)* Maybe I should leave.

(He rises.)

LILY. So storm out because you don't like my advice.

MICHAEL. Did you happen to detect a pattern in my collective social experiences?

LILY. Yes, poor judgement!

MICHAEL. No, rotten people!

LILY. You found what you were looking for.

MICHAEL. That's a cruel and facile thing to say. I'm not looking for crummy people in my life!

LILY. Then you found them by default looking for what you *really* wanted — a roll in the hay!

MICHAEL. The bullshit meter's going wild now! Thanks for the coffee.

(He crosses to the door.)

LILY. *(Rising)* Or you found them trying to avoid what you're afraid of -- intimate contact.

(MICHAEL stops and turns.)

MICHAEL. You really don't get out enough to evaluate my social interaction. Where's *your* bevy of wonderful friends?

LILY. I'm an old woman; most of them have died off.

MICHAEL. Oh, how convenient.

LILY. Besides, I can't even drive at night.

MICHAEL. That is so feeble.

LILY. Well I can't!

MICHAEL. If your night vision is bad, make some day friends!

LILY. I have friends!

MICHAEL. Please. You're as reclusive and anti-social as I am!

LILY. Nobody could be!

MICHAEL. You ate all by yourself in Morocco, remember?! Cous-cous, belly dancers, and screaming tourists — and there's Lily sitting alone in the corner behind a folding screen like the Sultan's favorite.

(LILY seems to submit to MICHAEL'S accusation. She speaks from the heart.)

LILY. It's hard to be alone, but it's harder for me to be with people. I get nervous, and I start to weigh every word, and, later, I regret half of what I've said and feel I've made a fool of myself. I'm just too self-conscious.

MICHAEL. I understand, Lily.

LILY. But I don't feel that way with you.

MICHAEL. Thank you. Neither do I.

LILY. Maybe because you don't weigh *anything* you say.

MICHAEL. I'm feeling a little less flattered now.

LILY. And God knows you spend half your time with your foot in your mouth.

MICHAEL. Okay. Made your point.

LILY. *(Smiling)* Okay. I had a lovely time tonight.

MICHAEL. Get out.

LILY. Thanks for the Cha-Cha steps.

MICHAEL. You already had the basics. Want to try the under-arm turn one last time to lock it?

LILY. *(Brightly)* Yes, but...*(Pointing downstairs.)* Ida.

MICHAEL. No music. I'll just count it out. *(He crosses to*

LILY and takes her in his arms.) Okay...start with the basic step —
    LILY. *(Following)* Okay...

MICHAEL. Back on your right foot, *cha-cha-cha*, then side, two, *cha-cha-cha*, and now the turn — *(But before they can complete the turn, the PHONE RINGS.)* My God, the woman's a human seismograph!

LILY. *(Crossing to phone.)* I knew she had been too quiet. *(Picking up receiver.)* Hello, Ida....*(Then, embarassed.)* Oh, I'm sorry, Robert.... *(Cupping receiver, sotto to MICHAEL.)* It's Ida's son. We're in deep shit now. *(MICHAEL grimaces. LILY, into receiver:)* No, it's not too late — we just came in....*(Then, serious.)* What, Robert...? *(LILY gasps.)* Oh my God, Robert. I'm so sorry. I'm so very sorry... *(MICHAEL crosses to LILY with concern.)* Yes, please let me know.... Good night.

(LILY absently replaces the receiver.)

    MICHAEL. What is it?
    LILY. Ida died in her sleep.
    MICHAEL. Oh my —
    LILY. Two nights ago. Here I was having this whole mental argument with her, and she was gone.
    MICHAEL. It's alright, Lily. It's alright.
    LILY. *(Through tears.)* Oh, I'm sorry. I'm just so sorry....

(As MICHAEL takes LILY in his arms and comforts her, FORE GROUND LIGHTS DIM and CHA-CHA MUSIC* RISES as the two stand embraced in silhouette against the NIGHT BACKDROP. Then, TOTAL BLACKOUT as CHA-CHA MUSIC FADES OUT, and:)

---

*For information regarding music use, please see page 85

WEEK SIX — CONTEMPORARY DANCE

(DAWN BACKDROP FADES IN as an upbeat sixties SURF TUNE
*RISES. FOREGROUND LIGHTS RISE — to reveal that the
room is partially configured for a dance lesson — and BACK-
DROP RISES TO BRIGHT MID-DAY with blue skies and
sparkling sea, as the SURF TUNE HITS FULL THROTTLE.
SURF TUNE FADES OUT as DOORBELL RINGS. No response.
DOORBELL RINGS AGAIN. No response again. Then knock-
ing at the door and:)

MICHAEL. *(OS)* Hello! Lily, I know you're home! *(He*
RINGS DOORBELL again. LILY enters from the left hallway. She
appears slightly disoriented and disheveled. As MICHAEL knocks
again, she gets her bearings and crosses to the door.) God, it's so
quiet in there you could hear a mouse fart!...Lily, all the neighbors
are opening their doors and staring!

LILY. For heaven's sake, what a racket!

(She opens the door, and MICHAEL bursts in wearing sunglasses,
a Hawaiian shirt, chinos, and tennis shoes and carrying his
tote.)

---

*For information regarding music use, please see page 85

MICHAEL. I knew mentioning the neighbors would do the trick. Hermits are just social butterflies without wings.

(LILY peers into the hallway before closing the door.)

LILY. Michael, I can't take all this rambunctiousness.

MICHAEL. What's wrong with you? *(Lifting his sunglasses.)* You look like the senior version of *Lost Weekend.*

LILY. *(Crossing to the rattan chair and sitting.)* I'm just feeling a little fragile today.

MICHAEL. Well, pick another day. It's Contemporary Dance day!

LILY. I don't know if I can take Contemporary Dance today.

MICHAEL. Kill joy.

LILY. Big mouth.

MICHAEL. You look all rumpled, like you slept in your clothes.

LILY. I got back from an appointment and was very tired and fell asleep, okay?!

MICHAEL. Okay. *(Clapping his hands.)* Wake up!

LILY. Michael, you're too *loud* — and so's your shirt!

MICHAEL. Oh, I'm rubber and you're glue. The shirt's to help set the mood, which I'm not going to let you ruin. *(He removes the CD player from his tote.)* I brought my Beach Boys CD for Contemporary Dance.

LILY. Beach Boys? I don't know how you define *contemporary.* The Beach Boys broke up at least twenty years ago. I saw on *Access Hollywood* that one of them was in rehab for ages--

MICHAEL. Alright, alright! Compared to Johann Strauss, they're "today"! *(He begins rolling up the carpet.)* And the tempo is perfect for several contemporary dances, many of which are hybrids of the Jive, Swing, or Jitterbug.

(LILY puts her foot on the carpet to stop MICHAEL.)

LILY. Look, seriously, Michael, I don't have the energy to do any of those jiggly dances today.

MICHAEL. Look, seriously, Lily, have a cup of coffee and tighten your bra strap.

LILY. I don't have to dance if I don't want to!

MICHAEL. Well you might as well, because you're paying for it either way!

LILY. Well I choose the no-dance way! *(Crossing to desk.)* Where's my checkbook?!

MICHAEL. Oh, there's the grand gesture again! Lady Rothschild cracks open her checkbook and the peasants hide their eyes to avoid being blinded.

LILY. *(Writing check, undaunted.)* Today's the ninth, right?

MICHAEL. I'm not telling you.

LILY. Let's see, what was that, fifty dollars?

MICHAEL. Fifty dollars for the lesson — and an additional thousand for pain and suffering.

LILY. Make that ten thousand for mine, but we'll call it even.

(LILY finishes writing the check, tears it from the book, and holds it out to MICHAEL, who stares at her without moving.)

MICHAEL. You'll have to hand it to me. I'm not going to go fetch it.

(LILY considers, then crosses to MICHAEL and holds the check out to him.)

LILY. Here...

MICHAEL. I won't accept it. You'll have to stuff it in my G-string like you're tipping a stripper.

(MICHAEL bends over to expose his rear pants pocket. LILY extends her hand to put the check in MICHAEL'S pocket, but is unable to complete the gesture.)

LILY. Oh, I can't do that! Just take it, would you!
MICHAEL. No, Lily, if you want to end it impersonally, let's really do it.
LILY. Oh, you impossible man! Even saying goodbye is difficult with you!

(LILY crosses past MICHAEL, drops the check on the coffee table, and sits on the couch. MICHAEL stares at LILY for a moment, then:)

MICHAEL. Is that what this is about?
LILY. Of course. It's the last lesson, isn't it?
MICHAEL. I told you I'd see you again.
LILY. You were just throwing an old dog a bone.
MICHAEL. I went to Ida's funeral with you, didn't I?!
LILY. That's only because you killed her.
MICHAEL. I thought we settled that!
LILY. Okay, we *both* killed her!
MICHAEL. That's better.

(LILY gets suddenly morose.)

LILY. Poor old thing. All I did was argue with her.
MICHAEL. I can relate to that.
LILY. I tormented her —
MICHAEL. Sounds familiar.

LILY. And then I chided her when all she was asking for was --

MICHAEL. *(Finishing for her.)* A little peace and quiet! God, Lily, set it to music.

LILY. Heartless! Nothing's sacred to you.

MICHAEL. *(Crossing to couch and sitting beside her.)* Come on, Lily. Ida enjoyed arguing with you. That's why she called you — it revved her engine. Who knows — your arguments probably extended her life by months.

LILY. *(Considering this.)* Robert did say, at the service, that she always spoke fondly of me.

MICHAEL. Oh, that was just funeral feel-good talk.

LILY. So why ruin it for me?!

MICHAEL. In the interest of reality! He said the same thing to me, and I never even met her!

LILY. He was trying to be nice. He's a very nice young man. I saw him looking at you. I think he may be, you know...gay.

MICHAEL. What makes you — you know — say that?

LILY. Well, for a man his age he's very trim and he has a full head of hair.

MICHAEL. Oh good, we found a cure for obesity and baldness. We already knew it worked to prevent pregnancy.

LILY. No, it's not just that. Ida told me that he wasn't married — because he couldn't find the *right girl.*

MICHAEL. Right. One with a penis.

LILY. So *you* think so, too?

MICHAEL. I didn't need the secret handshake to spot that one.

LILY. So why did you question it when *I* said it?

MICHAEL. I just wanted to explore your reasoning — based almost entirely on a false stereotype.

LILY. I don't claim to be an expert. You're the only gay man I've known —

MICHAEL. That's what you think —

LILY. *(Continuing)* Known *well!* And I hope you're not a representative sample!

MICHAEL. Really? What would be your *dream* sample?

LILY. Someone less *exasperating,* perhaps?

MICHAEL. Look, if you need to insult me to relieve your separation anxiety —

LILY. I wasn't insulting —

MICHAEL. Maybe I should make it easy for you and just go.

LILY. If you want to...

(MICHAEL rises abruptly, crosses to the CD player, packs it into his tote, and zips it up with finality.)

MICHAEL. I thought I could joke you out of this mood, but now I'm in it with you, and you're making me dance way too hard. I'm tired of dodging bullets. *(Crosses back to LILY and extends his hand, professionally.)* Goodbye, Lily.

LILY. *(Rising and taking his hand awkwardly.)* Oh...goodbye.

MICHAEL. It's been a pleasure teaching you, and getting to know you. You may be my first pupil, but I think you'll always be my best.

LILY. Well, thank you. *(Retrieving check from coffee table.)* Here's...this.

MICHAEL. *(Accepting check.)* Thank you. *(Continuing from the scripted lesson plan.)* And if Six Dance Lessons can be of any further service to you, please don't hesitate to call on us. If a dance has a name, we teach it. We have many qualified instructors.

(MICHAEL crosses to the door.)

LILY. I don't think I'd want another instructor; I was quite satisfied with the one I had.

MICHAEL. Thank you.

(As his hand touches the doorknob:)

LILY. Oh, Michael, how could you?!

MICHAEL. What?

LILY. Just give up like that.

MICHAEL. How much patience am I expected to have?!

LILY. A little more. How could you go all cold and professional on me?

MICHAEL. You're wearing me out, Lily!

LILY. See? I knew it.

MICHAEL. Knew what?

LILY. That you couldn't take it. I knew it wouldn't last. People don't have the patience to put up with people.

MICHAEL. *Difficult* people.

LILY. That's redundant! But I understand. If you thought it was bad now, maybe you *should* go.

MICHAEL. *(Confused)* What does that mean?

LILY. Nothing. *(Then, formally)* I'll call if I require further instruction. Thank you for satisfying my dancing needs.

(MICHAEL begins to leave, then turns back into the room.)

MICHAEL. Alright, do you want to have this goddamn Contemporary Dance lesson or not?

LILY. If you want to.

MICHAEL. Do *you* want to?!

LILY. *(Shrugging)* Maybe.

MICHAEL. Oh for God's sake!

LILY. So stop stalling and teach me already!

MICHAEL. I'll take that as an unqualified "yes!"
LILY. What do you want to drink?!
MICHAEL. Just some fuckin' water, please!
LILY. One fuckin' water, comin' up!

(As LILY enters the kitchen and pours a glass of water, MICHAEL appeals to the heavens, then unzips his tote and plugs in the CD player.)

MICHAEL. As I said, all contemporary dances share a common structural root. But they also share a philosophical root — and that is an anti-establishment freedom of expression through freedom of movement.

(LILY enters from the kitchen with MICHAEL'S water.)

LILY. Get out your shovels.
MICHAEL. It's a historical fact! *(LILY smiles as MICHAEL takes his glass and reaches into his pocket. He takes some pills from a plastic vial and pops them into his mouth. LILY looks on with some concern as MICHAEL washes down his pills.)* Now, what this means is less rigid foot patterns and more intricate hand movements. *(Removing footprints from tote and tossing them on the floor.)* But we'll start with the basic steps for Rock & Roll and move from there into the Monkey — *(Tosses more footprints.)* Twist, Hitchhike — *(Tosses more footprints.)* Swim, Jerk, Pony, Hustle... Oh, what the hell —

(Michael just throws the rest of the footprints on the floor in a jumble.)

LILY. Free expression!

MICHAEL. Exactly! *(He flips on the CD player. As SURF TUNE* RISES, MICHAEL crosses to LILY. They stand facing each other.)* Let's start with a *basic disco* or *freestyle* step, no hold--*(Lily follows as:)* Right foot to side, feet together, right again, turn and tap. Now the same on the left side. Left, together, left, turn and tap. That's it. Now let's add some — *(But before MICHAEL can add arm movements, LILY begins churning her forearms. Realizing she is anticipating the instruction, she throws MICHAEL a sly look, which he returns with a smile:)* Arms and some hip movements — stay with me now! We've left the realm of intellect and are into pure animal instinct! Let's *Monkey! (LILY follows adroitly and without inhibition.)* Good! Now arms and legs in opposition and *Twist! (The two Twist for a few measures before MICHAEL turns DS and begins to Hitchhike.)* Now just arms and hips and *Hitchhike! (LILY turns DS and follows without missing a beat.)* Travel! *(They cross and change places while Hitchhiking.)* There you go! Now *Hitchhike* with *attitude! (LILY assumes her haughtiest attitude.)* That's it! Now, be cool and *Swim! (LILY Swims.)* Do you know the *backstroke?! (LILY backstrokes like a champion, but begins to appear winded. She falls back into a chair. Unaware, MICHAEL continues:)* And that becomes the Jerk! Now the Pony! And *follow me! (MICHAEL Travel-Ponies around the sofa solo for a few measures before realizing that LILY is seated, catching her breath. He crosses to the CD player and SHUTS THE MUSIC.)* Oh, Lily, you should have stopped me.

LILY. *(Between breaths.)* That's okay, I knew you'd notice eventually.

MICHAEL. I'm sorry.

LILY. No, it was fun.

MICHAEL. Are you alright? Can I get you a glass of water?

---

*For information regarding music use, please see page 85

LILY. Yes, please.

(As MICHAEL crosses to kitchen.)

MICHAEL. You faked me out again. I thought you didn't have any experience with Contemporary Dance.

LILY. Well, my daughter taught me some steps years ago. I didn't think any of it had stuck. It was right before...

(MICHAEL returns with water, and offers the glass to LILY as he sits beside her.)

MICHAEL. I see.

(LILY takes the glass and sips.)

LILY. Thank you.

MICHAEL. She taught you well.

LILY. It was during her last break from college. Oh, we had so much fun. We'd roll up the carpet — *(Indicating floor.)* Just like this — after Harlan went to bed, and turn on the music real low, and we'd dance and laugh.

MICHAEL. Don't want to wake Harlan up.

LILY. *(Shaking her head emphatically.)* No.

MICHAEL. Now...was he really alive then?

LILY. Boy was he. Nan and I were always walking on eggshells around him. Nan loved her father, but I think she was always a little afraid of him. Maybe I was, too. *(MICHAEL nods.)* Would you like to see a picture of her?

MICHAEL. Of course I would.

(LILY crosses to her desk and reaches for a gold-leaf box nestled between her books. She opens it and removes an elaborately framed photograph.)

LILY. I keep it in here because if I leave it out, it stops me, pulls me right back.

MICHAEL. I understand.

(She crosses to MICHAEL and hands him the picture.)

LILY. You'd think after thirty years...

MICHAEL. *(Examining picture.)* What a beautiful girl, Lily.

LILY. She was, wasn't she? I don't think she was conscious of how beautiful she was.

MICHAEL. How did she —

LILY. *(Quickly)* It was an accident.

MICHAEL. Car?

LILY. No...complications from a surgical procedure.

MICHAEL. Oh — how terrible.

LILY. Actually, it was an abortion. An illegal abortion — of course; they all were then.

MICHAEL. Did you know she was pregnant?

LILY. Yes, she told me. She told me everything. But I made the mistake of telling Harlan. He turned to fire, then to ice. He forbad me to speak to her, and, like a good Baptist wife, I deferred to my husband's wishes. I don't know what he thought it would accomplish — the silent treatment for pregnancy, a new form of religious contraception. I told myself that he would come around, that the silence would end. But it didn't end quickly enough for Nan.

MICHAEL. It wasn't your fault, Lily.

LILY. Of course it was. I was her mother! It was my duty to protect her.

MICHAEL. You tried.

LILY. No, I turned from her in silence — as my husband told me to.

MICHAEL. Then you have to forgive yourself.

LILY. *(Shaking her head.)* No. After Nan's funeral, Harlan told me he prayed every night for God to wash her soul clean. That was his big belated father's gift to her — posthumous prayer. I told him to save his prayers for himself. I told him I hoped God had enough energy to wash *his* shriveled, sanctimonious soul clean! He looked at me as if he would strike me, and then he began to cry. You know, I think he actually expected me to console him. But I just left the room — I turned from *him* in silence, too. We both mourned for our daughter — but in separate rooms.

MICHAEL. My God, Lily, how did you get through it?

LILY. I never got through it — I just went around it. I got my teaching degree and began to work. And Harlan and I managed to stay together — a little like a broken pitcher that's been glued back together but can never hold water again.

MICHAEL. I'm sorry, Lily. I go through life as if I were the only person with nerve endings — and you've had so much pain.

LILY. No more than most. We're all walking past something. Look at you with your mother, and your Florida —

MICHAEL. *(Smiling)* Dates from hell.

LILY. Yes, not to mention New York.

MICHAEL. New York was the best time of my life. That's what's so unmentionable about it — the loss of it.

LILY. Your career, you mean?

MICHAEL. No, my friend Charlie — my love — died in New York. Afterward, his family treated me kind of badly.

LILY. I'm sorry, Michael.

MICHAEL. Hey — now I can remember Charlie and smile. Just as I know he's smiling at all my bad dates. Maybe he's *responsible* for them. Maybe that's his way of telling me you only get one good one.

LILY. That's not true. You might have to pass a million faces before you find another one — the special one. But you will.

MICHAEL. I might have to change states again, too.... Thanks, Lilly.

(LILY nods, rises, crosses to the desk, and returns the photo to the box. MICHAEL begins gathering the footprints from the floor. LILY turns tentatively to him.)

LILY. Michael, may I ask you something?

MICHAEL. Sure.

LILY. Are you sick?

MICHAEL. You mean mentally? I thought we'd already established that.

LILY. *(Smiling, then gently.)* I mean physically. Do you have...AIDS?

MICHAEL. *(Indignant)* What makes you ask that, Lily?

LILY. Your friend dying —

MICHAEL. Charlie died of pancreatic cancer, Lily. We do die of other diseases. What else?

LILY. Those "vitamins" you take —

MICHAEL. They're really vitamins. What else?

LILY. Your anger —

MICHAEL. Lily, I've got Pat Robertson, Jerry Falwell, Trent Lott, and the entire Family Research Council; I don't need AIDS to make me angry!

LILY. I'm sorry — I've offended you.

MICHAEL. Well, there's that stereotype again! Don't broadcast your ignorance too widely.

LILY. Oh, don't turn on me. I was concerned about you.

MICHAEL. I don't assume, because you're over seventy, that *you're* sick or dying.

LILY. I am.

MICHAEL. What...?

LILY. Sick or dying. I was diagnosed with lymphoma three years ago. I went into remission — until two weeks ago, when I got the lab report I'd been dreading. I've been driving to Morton Plant Hospital in Clearwater three times a week for radiation treatments.

MICHAEL. Oh, Lily...

LILY. That's why I get so tired.

MICHAEL. And I made you *dance.* Why didn't you tell me?

LILY. Because I *wanted* you to make me dance, I guess. Then there's my pride; I didn't want you to see me as a sick old woman.

MICHAEL. That's why you were pushing me out the door today, isn't it?

LILY. I suppose. After what you went through with your mother, I didn't want you to feel...obligated, in any way.

MICHAEL. Well, I do Lily. That's the litmus test for friendship -- a sense of obligation.

LILY. Well don't.

MICHAEL. Too late. In fact, when's your next treatment?

LILY. Friday, but —

MICHAEL. Because Morton Plant's right near my house. I could drive you there, and you could rest at my place afterward.

LILY. No, see, that's not what I wanted.

MICHAEL. No — that's not what you wanted to *admit* you

wanted. It'll be fun. We'll drink lemonade on the screen porch and listen to CD's. I'll pick you up at...?

(Pause, as LILY considers, then:)

> LILY. *(Shyly)* Ten-thirty?
> MICHAEL. *(Smiling)* It's a date.

(He takes LILY'S hands.)

> MICHAEL. You're going to be alright, Lily.

(LILY speaks in an anxious little voice.)

> LILY. Do you think so, Michael?
> MICHAEL. Oh, I know it. I can tell by the way you move. Speaking of which... *(MICHAEL rises and crosses to the CD player.)* We haven't finished our lesson.
> LILY. No, I don't think I could —

(MICHAEL flips on the CD player, and, as the SURF TUNE* RISES, he begins dancing toward LILY.)

> MICHAEL. Come on, Beach Bunny! Who could resist that beat? *(LILY shakes her head "no," but MICHAEL continues to beckon her.)* Let's go, surf's up! *(After a moment, LILY smiles, rises and joins MICHAEL.)* That's it!

(As MICHAEL begins to Hustle, LILY follows, smiling, as FORE-GROUND LIGHTS DIM, leaving them dancing in silhouette before the LIGHTED BACKDROP. As they dance off, SURF TUNE FADES and BACKDROP CHANGES TO NIGHT, THEN DAY, THEN LATE AFTERNOON, and QUICK TRAN-SITION to:)

---

*For information regarding music use, please see page 85

WEEK TEN — BONUS LESSON

(As BACKDROP CHANGES TO LATE AFTERNOON ON A CLEAR DAY, a sweet SURF BALLAD* RISES. FOREGROUND LIGHTS RISE — furniture and carpet are not arranged for a dance lesson — and keys jangle outside the front door.
SURF BALLAD FADES OUT as MICHAEL enters — alone. He stares at the empty room for a moment, then:)

MICHAEL. Here we are, safe and sound.

(MICHAEL turns to help LILY, who enters behind him. She appears much frailer and walks with some difficulty. MICHAEL watches protectively as she crosses to the couch.)

LILY. Sanctuary. It's good to be back.
MICHAEL. Do you want to go to your bedroom?
LILY. No, I'd rather stay out here with you.
MICHAEL. I'll still be here when you wake up.
LILY. No, I want to sit and watch the sun set with you.
MICHAEL. Good.

---

*For information regarding music use, please see page 85

(MICHAEL eases LILY into the couch as the BACKDROP SKY BEGINS TURNING A VIBRANT PINK.)

LILY. Thank you.
MICHAEL. How about some lemonade?

(MICHAEL begins tucking an afghan over LILY'S legs.)

LILY. Maybe later. *(Slapping MICHAEL'S hand.)* Relax now. You don't have to make a fuss over me!

(MICHAEL playfully slaps LILY back.)

MICHAEL. Okay! *(As Michael sits in the chair opposite her:)* So the doctor was encouraging today.
LILY. *(Shrugging)* People always give you something you want — in my case, hope — to sell you something you don't — in my case, systematic medical torture.
MICHAEL. Lily, the treatments have been very effective. You have to stay —
LILY. Positive. Yes, you're right. Look at the sky. *(The two turn upstage and look out the picture window as the SUNSET EXPLODES IN DEEP REDS AND ORANGES.)* The last part of the sunset's the best, don't you think? *(MICHAEL nods.)* Just when you think it's over, the sun throws its brightest colors all across the sky. The sunsets have been so *vibrant* lately.
MICHAEL. It's the time of year.
LILY. Or my time of life. Everything becomes more precious when we're running out of it.
MICHAEL. How morbid. Lily —
LILY. I know —
LILY and MICHAEL. *(In unison.)* Positive!

(The PHONE RINGS.)

MICHAEL. Want me to get that?
LILY. Please. I think it's for you, anyway.

(MICHAEL crosses to the phone.)

MICHAEL. For me? *(Lifting receiver.)* Hello...? Oh, hi, Robert....*(LILY smiles and nods playfully at MICHAEL, who waves her away.)* Yes, we just got back.... She's fine — strong as an old plow horse.
LILY. A simple "horse" would have sufficed. Ask him if he wants to come up for lemonade and sunset.
MICHAEL. Uh, Lily wants to know if you'd like to come up for lemonade and sunset.... Great, see you then. *(MICHAEL hangs up the receiver and turns to LILY. He tries to conceal his obvious pleasure.)* He's going to change from work and be up in a few minutes.

(LILY smiles and nods facetiously again.)

LILY. Good...
MICHAEL. Oh, stop it! You're in overdrive with this match-making thing.

(He crosses to the kitchen, removes three glasses and a tray from the pantry and a pitcher of lemonade from the refrigerator.)

LILY. I haven't done a thing!
MICHAEL. Yes, you have. You're always dropping hints and invitations.
LILY. I'm sorry you don't trust your own powers of attraction. Robert likes you very much — and you like him. Admit it.
MICHAEL. *(Grudgingly)* He's very nice, but —
LILY. No "buts" after "very nice." Robert won't be pushing you out of any moving vehicles.

MICHAEL. *(Crossing to coffee table with lemonade tray.)*
And we all know that's the primary criterion for my dream date.
LILY. Robert could be the one, Michael.
MICHAEL. Oh, come on —
LILY. Allow for the possibility. He could be the millionth face
you pass. The special one.

(MICHAEL stops and regards LILY quietly for a moment, then:)

MICHAEL. I think that was you, Lily.

(LILY looks at MICHAEL and fights to hold back her tears.)

LILY. Thank you, Michael....
MICHAEL. How about a little dance with me at sunset?
LILY. No, I don't think I —
MICHAEL. Come on. Just a slow one —

*(MICHAEL flips on the CD player and chooses a cut. He crosses to
LILY as the SURF BALLAD* RISES.*
*MICHAEL takes LILY'S hand and lifts her into his arms. The two begin
to dance — so gracefully, you might not notice that LILY'S feet are
barely touching the floor.*
SURF BALLAD RISES, and LILY rests her head on MICHAEL'S
shoulder as they continue to dance — and their dance hold evolves
into a warm embrace. Then FOREGROUND LIGHTS DIM leaving LILY and MICHAEL dancing in silhouette before a BRIL-
LANT RED AND ORANGE SUNSET. As the SKY DARKENS, a
SHOOTING STAR PIERCES THE SKY and:)*

CURTAIN FALLS SLOWLY

---

*For information regarding music use, please see page 85

The following songs and recordings were utilized in the Broadway production of "Six Dance Lessons in Six Weeks" at the Belasco Theater in New York City in the fall of 2003:

"Bei Mir Bist Du Schoen" by Winfried Luessenhop, Jacob Jacobs, and Sholom Sholen Secunda. **Music publishing rights:** Warner Chappell Music, Inc., 10585 Santa Monica Blvd., Los Angeles, CA 90025, Attn.: Theatrical Licensing Department, 310-441-8600; **Sound recording rights:** Universal Music, 100 Universal City Plaza, Building 1440-13, Universal City, CA 91608, Attn.: Film and Music TV Dept., 310-865-5000.

"Blue Tango," music by Leroy Anderson, lyrics by Mitchell Parish. **Music publishing rights:** EMI Entertainment World, 810 Seventh Avenue, New York, NY 10019, Attn.: Music Services Licensing, 212-830-5155; **Sound recording rights:** BMG Special Products, 8750 Wilshire Blvd., Beverly Hills, CA 90211, 310-358-4016.

"Laughing Song" by Johann Strauss, English lyrics by Mel Mandel and Norman Sachs.

"The Best is Yet to Come" by Carolyn Leigh & Cy Coleman. **Music publishing rights:** EMI Entertainment World, 810 Seventh Avenue, New York, NY 10019, Attn.: Music Services Licensing, 212-830-5155, and Warner Chappell Music, Inc., 10585 Santa Monica Blvd., Los Angeles, CA 90025, Attn.: Theatrical Licensing Department, 310-441-8600.

"La Ultima Noche" by Roberto (Bobby) Collazo. **Music publishing rights:** Peer Music III Ltd., 810 Seventh Avenue, New York, NY 10019, 212-265-3910.

"Surfin' USA" by Chuck Berry. **Music publishing rights**: Arc Music Corporation and Isalee Music, 254 West 54th Street, 13th Floor, New York, NY 10019, 212-246-3333; **Sound recording rights:** EMI Capitol Records, 5750 Wilshire Blvd., Suite 300, Los Angeles, CA 90036, 323-692-1132.

"God Only Knows" by Brian Douglas Wilson and Tony Asher. **Music publishing rights:** Universal Music, 2440 Sepulveda Blvd., Suite 100, Los Angeles, CA 90064, 310-235-4800; **Sound recording rights:** EMI Capitol Records, 5750 Wilshire Blvd., Suite 300, Los Angeles, CA 90036, 323-692-1132.

No rights to the above songs and recordings have been acquired for purposes other than the Broadway production. For further information about the use of these songs and recordings, please contact the music publishers with respect to the songs and the record companies with respect to the recordings.

Costume Plot

Michael Minetti

Throughout
- tee shirt
- black socks

Scene 1
- black pants
- blue striped shirt
- black belt
- black dance oxfords

Scene 2
- repeat pants, belt, shoes
- black stretch shirt
- black waist sash
- red neck scarf

Scene 3
- repeat pants, belt, shoes
- white pleated shirt
- black bow tie
- black tux jacket

Scene 4
- repeat pants, belt, shoes
- white shirt
- red tie
- black/white houndstooth jacket
- black fedora

Scene 5
- repeat pants, shoes
- white shirt w/ black ruffles
- white braces
- black cumberbun
- black hand tie bow tie
- silver dinner jacket

Scene 6
- khakis
- hawaiian shirt
- tan belt
- tan loafers
- sunglasses

Scene 7
- repeat pants, belt, shoes
- blue silk shirt

Costume Plot

Lily Harrison
Throughout
    wedding ring
    pantyhose

Scene 1
    orange dress
    yellow floral jacket
    peach flats

Scene 2
    2 pc blue pant suit
    floral scarf
    ocelot flats

Scene 3
    peach waltz gown
    peach pumps

Scene 4
    green plaid bathrobe
    white flannel nightgown
    slippers

then
    white dress
    black jacket w/ pearl brooch
    pearl earrings
    black pumps

Scene 5
    2 pc burgundy silk pantsuit
    pink kimono
    wine earrings and necklace
    cocktail ring
    wine flats

Scene 6
    tan pants
    blue stripe linen shirt
    tan loafers

Scene 7 repeat pants
    yellow blouse
    beige flats

Property Plot

DR AREA:
LIGHT SWITCH "ON"
Swivel chair, facing SL
Square glass-top table on spike, with...
    Candy jar US and 2-3 literary magazines DS
Wicker pouf stool on spike
RUG, rolled up, DR of stool

DESK / BOOKSHELVES:

Middle shelf	-square wicker box with photo of Nan, set face-up
Desktop	-small Kleenex box
Desk drawer	-checkbook with pen stuck inside (make sure at least two checks are inside)
By desk	-wooden chair with needlepoint cushion, on spike
	-trash can, empty, under desk

UR AREA:
Small plant on spike
Small wicker trunk with green throw, on spike

UL AREA:
Round glass-top table w/plant on top
White chairs to SR & SL of table, on spike

DL AREA:
Chaise and 2 throw pillows
Phone table, with...
    Phone (HUNG UP)
    address book with Seminole hospital list inside
    "Six Dance Lessons" ad on top of address book
Coffee table, with...
    3 magazines stacked on SL side
    small candy dish with Ricola on SR side
island toy

Kitchen Island Top:
WIPE TOP CLEAN
Creamer & sugar on holder
Coffee maker
Salt/pepper shakers
Napkin holder with at least 10 napkins
"Placemat" towel
hand towel, folded
metal utensil box with (DS to US...)
     2 soup spoons (upside down,) 4 coffee spoons, 2 forks
Kleenex box, make sure no tissues popping out

Kitchen Island shelf:
2 bowls on top of...
2 small plates
6 coffee cups/saucers
cookie jar with some oatmeal
    raisin cookies inside
small jar at least 1/2 full of decaf
8 small water glasses

Kitchen Island bottom shelf: extra small glass or two
2 stools in front of island, spaced far apart

SINK:
Hot water canister full of hot water

FRIDGE:
Top of fridge   wicker tray
Inside fridge   pitcher 1/3 full of water
Top shelf   pitcher 1/2 full of lemonade
     2 pieces of "cake" on plates
     prop storage: lemonade mix & milk for creamer,
       extra cookies

OFFSTAGE LEFT:
Afghan
Kleenex box in box holder

OFFSTAGE RIGHT:
Tote bad #1, with...
    CD player #1
    "swing" footprint envelope with footprints and cheat card set
    in front of CD player

Tote bag #2, with...
    CD player #2
    "tango" footprint envelope with footprints and cheat card set
    in front of CD player

"Waltz" envelope with footprints & cheat card, small towel
"Foxtrotn envelope with footprints & cheat card, small towel
"Contemporary" envelope with footprints & cheat card,
    CD and towel

BY FRONT DOOR:
Pill bottle of vitamins
Set of house keys

IN GREEN ROOM CANTEEN:
Paper bags for soup
Soup containers and lids
Soup

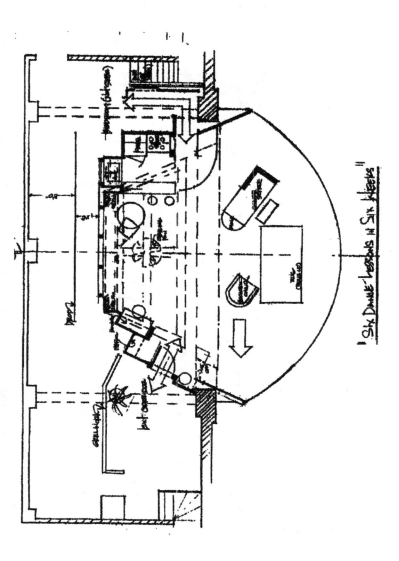